UNSETTLING STRANGERS

GW00419412

Unsettling Strangers

Jeremy Fonge

First edition—May 1995

ISBN 1 85902 114 X

Published with the support of the Arts Council of Wales.

Printed by J. D. Lewis & Sons Ltd, Gomer Press, Llandysul, Dyfed

Contents

Playing the Game

The alarm was raised by Dafydd Lewis, when, purely by chance, he noticed a pane of glass had been smashed in the back door of Felin Newydd.

'It was a nice morning, see?' he told Detective Inspector Ryan Morgan, who was in charge of the fire-bomb investigations, 'so I went down the bottom fields to see how the grass was coming on.'

His son was the last to go down that way—to spread some fertiliser. That was about ten days ago, but what with driving the tractor and keeping to his mark, it was unlikely he had had time to take a look at Felin Newydd.

'Do many people travel down the lane?' Morgan asked.

Lewis shrugged, looking out across the valley from his hill-top farmyard. Down in the bottom, amid riverside trees, policemen were quartering the acre of land behind Felin Newydd. Cars and vans, brilliant white and orange-striped, were parked hard against the hedges lining the narrow lane which ran past the former woollen mill.

'Not so many,' Lewis responded. 'See, the lane only comes up here and on down to Derwendeg and Dolau.'

'So, basically, it is only used by people visiting the farms?'

'That's about it.'

Lewis was a lean, dark, balding man in his mid-fifties; a wiry man, dedicated to his 250-acre Allt-y-Gog Farm and its 150 dairy cows. Morgan was a head taller and ten years younger, with the build of a prop forward and a head of thick, black, curly hair. He asked for a basic list of people who used the lane. Lewis appeared less concerned to set the record straight than the investigator.

'People come and go, see? Reps, lorry drivers—all sorts.'

'The people at Felin Newydd, Mr Lewis: how often did they come down?'

The other shrugged: 'Not this winter that I know of.'

'Only during the better months, then?'

1

'It seems that way.'

'Do you know them at all?'

Lewis moved to an old hay baler parked in the yard corner and sat on the bale chute. Morgan stood over him.

'Can't say I do.'

'Did you ever speak to them?'

'Once, twice maybe.'

'But they've had the place what? Ten, eleven years now?'

'About that.'

'And you never spoke to them?'

'She came up for some milk once.'

'Nothing more?'

'I saw him to say good morning off and on—that sort of thing.'

Morgan moved to obstruct the farmer's view of Felin Newydd.

'Were there any bad feelings or suchlike?'

Lewis offered up a mirthless smile: 'Na' boy—we just let them get on with it.'

And with that he stood and walked away.

At an impromptu press conference outside the former mill, an assistant chief constable announced: 'In this instance a device was discovered at the foot of the property's main staircase. I shudder to think what the outcome might have been had there been a fire with the family resident—a family involving three children aged three to eleven.'

David Vernon Thomas (popularly known as 'D.V.') smiled wryly as he made assiduous note of the ACC's every word. It was always the same with fire bomb attacks: there were too many 'ifs' and 'buts' floating about, and they always culminated in a great big 'might'. Did the ACC really believe his own words? In twenty to thirty years of holiday-home attacks, none of the police forebodings had come true. Places had burned down, but not with people in them. Whoever was behind the attacks, D.V. believed, was canny enough to go so far and not a fraction further.

Driving back up the lane to the nearest village, he decided to conduct a vox-pop of local opinion, to drum up a nice little 'what-the-people-think' piece to run alongside the main story.

'It's nasty, but it happens, see?' said an elderly lady outside the Post Office. 'People who buy these places, well, they know what goes on.'

She refused to give her name. How could D.V. explain that her answer was too blithe, too 'pat' to ring true?

A tractor driver, young, dark and slim, came out of the shop with packets of crisps and a bottle of pop in his hands.

'You'll not quote me, then?' he asked as D.V. pressed him for a comment.

'Of course not!'

The young man's smile was enigmatic.

'Shall I say it's a bad job, then? Shouldn't happen?'

Then he climbed into his cab and slammed the door.

The pub was newly-opened, the bar still empty.

'What do I reckon?' the landlord asked. There was a glint of mirth in his eyes. 'Well now, it's a damn fool thing, that's what I reckon.'

He was massively built, pot-bellied and bearded. D.V. lodged himself on a bar stool. He was slim, with lank brown hair. Thirty two and dressed like someone with little thought for clothes.

'Do you know the people at Felin Newydd?'

The landlord wiped the dry counter with a dry cloth.

'Doubt I'd know them in the street.'

'They don't have much to do with the village?'

'They're all the same, those people. Come down here when they please, swan around and go back when they please.'

'There's a few of them around here, then?'

'Some say too many.'

'Do you think so?'

The landlord turned to fiddle with the optic bottles.

'Maybe ... I'm not sayin' for sure ...' And then, over his shoulder, he added: 'Sometimes I think something ought to be done.'

D.V.'s thoughts dwelled on the landlord's eyes and he began to reflect on this all the more: the woman outside the post office, the young tractor driver—their mouths said one thing, their eyes another.

3

Back in the office it was the same with the Rev. Handel Williams as he sat and chatted over a cup of tea with the Editor.

'It's a highly dangerous practice, I must say that,' but his eyes said something else.

'Wind it up a bit,' D.V.'s editor ordered, meaning 'turn out the usual shock, horror, front-page splash stuff.' Yet even he appeared entirely unruffled by the whole business, if not quietly amused.

Two days later, Ryan Morgan was in a bullish mood when he met D.V. for a lunchtime pint.

'I tell you, boy, it's beginning to all come together. There's the car, see? A blue or grey Vauxhall Nova seen parked by the mill place New Year time. Then . . . well . . .'

Morgan checked himself deliberately in an attempt to create the impression there was far more to go on than he was prepared to divulge.

There were, in fact, only two other pieces of evidence to work on: three minute fragments of fibre taken from the jagged glass of the broken window, and part of a footprint. The fibres, according to forensic, came from a dark blue, Marks and Spencer man's sweater, the footprint from a size eight Reebok trainer. Morgan laughed inwardly at the impossibility of it all.

'How many needles do you reckon?' D.V. asked, sitting back with his hands linked behind his head, as if to say 'speak freely'.

Morgan sniffed: 'Two, I suppose—one in the car keeping look out, the other doing the job.'

'And a haystack the size of Wales?' D.V. raised his eyebrows in an amused, speculative grimace.

Morgan responded with a sour smile and an excuse to leave immediately.

As he worked on the fire-bomb follow-up for the next week's issue, D.V. found himself writing that the police were still 'confidently pursuing several leads' during inquiries into an incident which had 'shocked the local community'.

He sat back and re-read his piece: a nice touch, people expected to read that sort of thing, and so did the police. As a local newspaper reporter, D.V. believed he carried the public conscience in such

4

matters. It was like adultery, he mused: it was best condemned in public, even though people all around enjoyed or yearned for the odd extra-marital dalliance.

Ryan Morgan read the piece with a hollow smile as he sat with D.V. in his office and pondered what to do next. He flicked through the rest of the paper, folded it up and laid it on his desk.

'So,' Morgan sat back, his hands linked in his lap, 'we're still in confident pursuit, then?'

D.V. was deadpan. 'One has to obey form in such matters.'

Morgan stretched and yawned. 'Well, what else can one do . . .?'

D.V. hooked his left ankle onto his right knee and settled the best he could on a hard, moulded plastic chair.

'Nothing solid yet?'

Morgan shrugged: 'Nothing that will get us anywhere fast.'

'There's the Vauxhall Nova,' D.V. offfered.

'Ha, ha, ha!' Morgan stood, hands in pockets, and propped his backside on the window ledge. 'Do you know how many blue, grey, blue-grey, silver, silver-blue, silver-grey, light blue, light grey, dark blue, dark grey Novas have been built in the last six or seven years?'

'Nope.'

'Then don't ask.'

'What about the locals?'

'Have you spoken to any?'

'A few.'

'And?'

'Have you ever seen a stripper in action, Ry? There she is, doing all the right things, winding all the men up and all with a great big smile on her face, but what are her eyes telling you? They're saying the audience is full of jerks and all she wants is to be home, tucked up in bed—alone.'

Morgan slumped back in his chair.

'I know what you mean, boy. They say all the right things but tell you sod all. That farmer Lewis, up the top, I reckon he was quietly laughing his socks off. The son too.'

D.V. decided to test Morgan some more.

'Of course, we assume the fire bombers were young men, but they don't have to be.'

Morgan raised an eyebrow, instantly wary: 'How do you mean?'

'That's the impression given—young, male hotheads.'

Morgan sniffed: 'Maybe.'

D.V. pressed a little harder. 'Well, I've seen you in trainers, Ry, and I bet the missus buys Marks and Sparks.'

Some of Morgan's junior officers had proved less circumspect about certain things than their boss. Morgan knew full well tongues were bound to wag.

'So?'

'An older man? A woman, perhaps.'

'How come?'

'There are some big girls about these days, Ry. You've got some in the station. So, they wear size eights and, on a chilly evening, a good, thick, man's sweater.'

Morgan sighed. D.V. was right. There were women constables about who had to wear size eights or nines—and it was not beyond his wife to wear one of his old sweaters for gardening.

'So what chance have we got then, D.V.?'

The reporter grinned: 'None?'

Both men sat in silence for a good thirty seconds or more, sipping machine-made coffee in waxed-cardboard cups.

'The thing is Ry, what did he—or she—actually do?'

Morgan decided to hedge, reflecting ruefully that detectives did not carry the sole right to deducing what may or may not have happened that night at Felin Newydd. He stood and lodged his backside against the windowsill again.

'You tell me, D.V.'

'Ok.' D.V. leant forward, elbows on knees. 'A small pane of glass was smashed and a bottle of petrol was placed at the foot of the stairs. What does that amount to?'

'Breaking and entering with intent to endanger life and property, attempted arson, attempted manslaughter—the book full.'

Morgan jingled coins in his pocket and took a pace out into the room and back again, watching D.V. all the while.

6

'Endangering life? Come on Ry! They knew the place was empty—had to. Where was the car? The Felin Newydd people weren't at a New Year's Eve party with three kids that young. Anyway, who would go round smashing door panes with people in the house? And then there's the eyes and mouths: the one thing they do say is that if anyone had been killed or injured, then God help the bombers—and the people you're after know it. They live among us, Ry—they know the score.'

'OK, OK,' Morgan waved a dismissive hand. 'The property then, and you're forgetting the matches. Somebody wanted the place burned down.'

D.V. shook his head and inspected the palms of his hands.

'Not this time, Ry. Would you throw lighted matches at a bottle of petrol?'

'These are hotheads—logic's not their forte.'

'Ha!' D.V. sat up and straightened his shoulders. 'Why not just stuff paper under the stairs and put a match to it? They went in, put the bottle down and scattered dead matches round it.'

Morgan sat down again: 'You reckon?'

'Put it this way: would you throw a lighted match at a bottle of petrol? If they had done that, then bang! You would have had your body. An own goal, the Army call it in Northern Ireland.'

Morgan scratched a heavy cheek, his nails rasping on a stubble already prominent after his morning shave. He surveyed D.V. carefully. The reporter was right, of course. Worse, he knew it. Whoever did the Felin Newydd job was trading on a latent public sympathy, but one fragile enough to turn the whole holiday home business on its head if ever there were a human casualty. Still, Morgan reflected, D.V. was a sensible chap. He would still co-operate: saying one thing, thinking another, doing a third, just to keep the front up. He and D.V. were both like D.V.'s stripper: they had to maintain the myth. He sighed.

'OK, D.V., you're not so daft, but you'll still play along, eh? Play the game?'

D.V. grinned: 'Damn, Ry, why not? It pays our wages, doesn't it?'

7

One Less Again

In the damp chill of a January afternoon, a small cluster of mourners moved away from Douglas Roberts's grave.

Delia Williams, watching from her cottage on the low hill behind the burial ground, experienced a pang of both concern and surprise that so few men had gathered to honour the death and internment of old Douglas. Beyond the twenty or so members of the choir, only a handful of others were present, all of them elderly in gloves and scarves and thick black coats, brought together to honour a man once considered a cultural lion within his community and much further afield.

Common gossip said it was Douglas's heart which had finally given out, having never fully recovered from an attack in October, when Douglas was found lying in great distress at the foot of the steps to the beach. Delia believed otherwise, remembering the evenings and afternoons spent with the old man on his return from hospital. In particular, that first afternoon, when he had spoken with such sadness.

'There'll be no more choir for me now, girl.'

And he had sighed and looked out the cottage window with tired blue eyes, down across the heather towards the beach and to where the waves were in lazy retreat from high tide. Gulls flapped and squabbled in the lowering light of that late-October day: Pen Stack was already lost from view amid the misty gloom beyond Maes Dewi headland. Almost stealthily, lights were beginning to show in the windows of the small white houses scattered round the bay. A lone, modern cruiser rocked at its moorings where once fishing craft had clustered.

'Don't be daft, Douglas, man! Another month and you'll be off down West Eynon singing with the best of them!'

Square-faced and square-built, Delia's very appearance added conviction to her every word and action, whatever her internal doubts.

8

The old man, thin and pale from illness, shifted his bony frame in the upright wing chair. Knobbly white ankles and a glimpse of long-johns showed beneath the scuffed turn-ups of baggy flannel trousers as he sought more comfort, tugging his blue-check dressing gown across his hollow chest as he did so. The heart attack had rid his once handsome face of its remaining charisma. Delia was disturbed by the blank eyes which once twinkled and laughed and held audiences captive throughout Douglas's beloved West Wales. She wondered for how much longer she would come and sit with him, talk of the past and maintain the tiny cottage in trim and tidy order.

His voice spoke of the present, his mind was in the past.

'No, girl, I'll not be going down there again.'

The choir was his last, now tenuous link with a once active and hectic life as a performer and celebrity in his old West Walian domain. He had told tales handed down through the centuries, written and recited his own poetry, sung the old songs and danced with a natural skill and grace bestowed on him by a sheer love of rhythm and an instinctive affinity with the pace and mood of music.

He had never seen the need to prove himself on a larger stage. Village concerts and Eisteddfodau were a joy to him as he mixed freely among people of his own kind. To Douglas, the National Eisteddfod existed for the intellectuals—academics, teachers, lecturers, ministers. Had he been a younger man, he might have mingled with them.

Douglas's roots were modest. After finishing school at twelve, he worked on a farm by day and read all he could by night. Thus he grew and matured and developed his considerable reputation. He was almost eighty when he decided it was time to cut back his activities to concerts with the West Eynon choir. Four years later he was now resigning himself to sitting at his cottage window, staring out over the tiny bay. Even his unswerving dedication to Bethel Chapel, amid the cluster of houses which formed the village of Cwmcae, appeared of little import.

Delia, twenty years Douglas's junior, rose to switch on the light and draw the curtains.

9

'There'll be somebody to give you a lift, sure to be,' she persisted, determined that he should not give up so quickly.

'It's not that, girl—it's not that. They'll be wanting new blood now, not the likes of me, hanging on, getting nowhere.'

'Damn it, man, do you think they'll throw out the likes of you? There's still more in you than half of them put together!'

Delia tugged at the hem of her cardigan to emphasise her point and sat back in the armchair opposite Douglas.

'Stop your chuntering now, woman—you know what I mean. Anyway, it's no sort of choir to be thinking of nowadays—twenty men where there were sixty, and who's coming along for the future, eh?'

Delia had no answer to that. Thirty years ago (or was it more?) the sixty choir members had lived almost exclusively within a five-mile radius of West Eynon. Now there were twenty five, and some travelled as many miles to attend the weekly practice. Some even lacked proper Welsh.

'Well,' Delia responded as stoutly as she could, 'there's plenty of men in the new houses at West Eynon—and on that little estate in Williams Street. There'll be some of them wanting to sing, sure to be.'

Douglas remained obdurate: 'If they'd have wanted to sing, woman, they'd have been with us before now.'

Delia, whose inclination was to do rather than think, blamed the choir's decline on television—on the modern preference for sitting in front of 'the box' and doing nothing. It was the same with the Women's Institute and Merched y Wawr—both were dominated by older women like her.

It was time for supper and as she prepared steamed cod in the small back kitchen, Delia realised with a shudder that she now knew more about the dead of the village than the living; the intricacies of ancient family relationships which no longer signified, the jobs people did, their behaviour and ways—their precise standing within the community. And not in Cwmcae alone, but in the villages around.

Rarely was Delia given to flights fo fancy, but for one moment she

10

was reminded of an old quilt found in Eunice Jones's tallboy after her death. Once rich in detail and colour, the quilt had faded with wear, the strength of the colour and design lost and fragmented. Life was like that now in the villages around.

Delia returned to the sitting room to find Douglas asleep. She switched on the radio, first ensuring the volume was low. From the speaker came the familiar, cheery voice of William Cary Williams, regaling his unseen audience with tales of his life as a broadcaster.

'And would you believe,' Williams was saying, his voice full of laughter, 'ten years later, while I was strolling along the Prom at Aberystwyth minding my own business, there came this little tap on my shoulder. Only a little one, mind, but did I jump? Damn, I jumped as high as my old Dad when Emlyn Jenkins let off a 12-bore shotgun two feet from Dad's left ear. Anyway, I jumped, as I said, and there was this little man smiling at me like an old friend from long ago . . .'

The story was drowned out by a growl of disgust from Douglas's bony frame.

'Calls himself a story teller? Ha! The only stories he tells are about himself. That's all they are, these broadcasting people—prattlers. Too fond of themselves and what they get up to, and can't say a thing unless it's about themselves or written on a script.'

Delia switched off the radio, and Douglas leaned forward to pick up a piece of cod going cold on a plate on a small table beside him.

'Stories,' he announced, a flake of cod quivering on his lower lip, 'are about other people: what they do, how they feel, what they think and how we see them—not about ourselves and what we get up to.'

'Aye, it's a shame,' Delia concurred quietly, 'but it's the way things are these days.'

She liked listening to Cary Williams. He cheered her up in the gloomy afternoons. She could potter round her house and listen to him without having to think about what he was saying.

'Change!' Douglas snorted, forgetting his meal for a moment. 'When people first started writing, did they write about themselves? 'Course they didn't! Even before Taliesin, people told tales of those

11

they admired and those they feared. Think of the old tales, woman: Branwen, Pwyll and Rhiannon, Saint David himself, Llewelyn, Giraldus. For centuries we've told tales of others, not of ourselves. But now it's all us: what we do, what we think, how we feel—not others.'

Delia let the matter drop, noting with satisfaction a glint of the old fire returning to Douglas's eyes.

True to the old custom that women did not attend funerals, Delia waited in her cottage, anxious that the mourners should enjoy the tea now waiting for them on her table.

Smiles of fond rememberance spread over elderly, weather-beaten faces as the dark-clad men began to talk more freely of Douglas and his life.

'You know that poem of his "How Will Our People?"' a thickset man with gold-rimmed spectacles asked of his companions. 'Well, he wrote it after he went to Llangollen International Eisteddfod for the first time.

'He was like a child, boys. Couldn't believe how all those youngsters from all over the world—even from places where countrymen were fighting countrymen—could be so caught up and dedicated to the thrill of it all.' The man chuckled. 'Damn, I can see Douglas now, standing there at the entrance of the pavilion late in the afternoon. It was hot, mind—one of the hottest days of the year —and on stage there was a group of Hungarian dancers. Outside a little French girl was singing, sitting on the grass with some friends. Somewhere a choir was warming up and nearby a gaggle of boys were arguing—some in Welsh, some in Breton and laughing all over their faces. Well, Douglas just stood there, with a smile from ear to ear in that old serge suit of his. The sweat was pouring off him and you could almost see him wanting to get up there on the stage himself. Then he turned to me and said "you know that song, Jones, *I'd like to teach the world to sing?* Well, damn me if there isn't something in it, eh?" Douglas did chuckle at that. One of our best poets this century and he was like a kid at Christmas. Aye,' the man sighed, 'it was after that that he wrote the poem, and if there were an anthem fit for the International, it had to be that.'

Delia was busy gathering up plates and cups and keeping the table tidy, but she did wonder for one brief moment for how long the unwritten tales of Douglas's life would survive. They lived even now within the memories of men growing old, and with the death of Douglas another strand of a great tradition going back to Celtic times had been broken.

Alone again after the mourners had gone she recalled another of those last, dwindling evenings with Douglas.

'When was it that they last danced down there, eh?' he had demanded, nodding towards the white sands of the bay. 'Willie with his pipes and Jackie on his old accordion and all the kids scrambling around the rock pools?' He fixed his gaze on Delia's impassive face with rheumy pale eyes. 'It was our beach once, you know. Now I look out in the summer and it's covered with strangers. Remember the cricket on the Morfa Field? Covered with cars now from June to September, and they say that's progress!'

Delia picked up her knitting and let the old man talk.

'Damn, they talk about how we're better educated and what do people do? Sit and watch the television and go drinking. Huh! Were those people who danced on the beach and who sang in the choir educated? 'Course not. Remember Myfanwy Davies, eh?' He shook his head in wonder. 'Out of school at twelve, seven children by the time she was thirty and she could dance the feet off every one of those kids you see on television.'

Delia had heard about Myfanwy. There had been some debate about the number of men required to sire the seven children. She wondered if Douglas was one of them, seeing as Buddug had died so young, along with his two little ones. Even Delia had entertained hopes of the once-dashing widower many years ago.

'Damn, woman,' Douglas grumbled on, 'the time was when there would be people in and out all the time. Aye, I was never short of company then, but who is there now, eh?'

Delia could find no answer. She wondered if Myfanwy was one of

13

those people. Douglas pressed on, working the answer out for himself.

'I'll tell you, then. How many houses are there in Cwmcae?'

Delia fiddled with her wedding ring: the ring she had accepted from Joseph after hopes of Douglas had faded.

'Twenty five, six?'

'Thirty one,' Douglas announced with blunt authority. 'Thirty one counting in every place you can see from the beach to the hill tops. And how many Welsh people live in them?'

Delia frowned. 'Now then—there's the Joneses at Pantgwyn, Thomases at Morfa Bach, Brynteg and Tŷ Newydd.' She was counting on her fingers. 'Pritchard Y Glyn, Sanders Tŷ Parc—that's six. And me and you and Enid Evans, of course.'

Delia puzzled some more, but that was enough for Douglas.

'Nine—and how many English?'

Delia drew in a deep breath and frowned again.

'Six, seven?'

'It's nine again.'

Delia nodded acceptance of that intelligence.

'So,' Douglas continued, 'what does that mean, eh?'

He sniffed and fixed his pale stare on Delia. 'It means there're thirteen houses sitting empty in this place most of the year. Getting on for half the houses in the bay—houses where people used to read and sing and write and then came down to the beach or hall or Chapel to share it all. And it's the same all along the coast—West Eynon, Williams Street and the rest. True they've built a few houses here and there, but it's not the same, woman.' He turned away from Delia and stared into a past which lay far beyond the glowing coal fire. 'No girl, sure as I'm sitting here, now I'm finished it's one less again for the choir. Aye, one less again . . .'

Only the busy clicking of Delia's needles broke the silence as Douglas slipped quietly into sleep. He died while Delia was preparing his supper.

In his will, Douglas stipulated that his papers and books be lodged with the National Library of Wales; that Buddug's harp—once owned by her grandmother—be given to the National Museum and

14

that the proceeds from the sale of his cottage and belongings be split equally between Delia, the Chapel and the International Eisteddfod, after the deduction of £2,000 for the West Eynon choir. As the will was read, it struck Delia that Douglas must once have considered this latter sum to be a major proportion of his assets. The cottage sold for £40,000 to a solicitor from Oxford, who brought in builders to double its size. His wife and children spent a week there after the work was completed, then no more was seen of them until the following spring. The gulls which pecked amid the tide wrack in the bay were more a part of the village.

And Delia knew this as she looked out across the bay at the empty house during those long autumn and winter months and found herself murmuring: 'Aye, Douglas old friend, it's one less again, and it's far more than the choir that misses you.'

Free of Hassle

Zac and Jake were late. They said they'd be back on Monday. It was now Wednesday. So Iretha hung around the caravan and waited, walked up and down the lane a bit and down to the village to cash her Giro. Or just sat on the 'van step and stared at the Preseli Hills. At night, she lay on her bed and smoked joints. They helped her drift off into fantasies which blocked out the loneliness. She knew Zac would be back. It wasn't the first time he'd stayed away like this.

Sylvie had called in yesterday, all bronzed and in one of her long, flowery cotton skirts. Earth Mother Sylvie, with her little blonde brats, stupid goats, flea-bitten hens and earthenware crockery. Silly bitch: all that home-made jam, yoghurt and bread stuff. And Robert fiddling about with his piddling 'crafts'. They were so middle class, Sylvie and Robert, so full of their kids learning Welsh. People only spoke Welsh around here when they wanted to be rude about the English.

Iretha didn't know why Sylvie kept calling. Didn't the silly cow realise she and Zac had come down here to get away from people like her, with silly middle class values? The silly cow had Sidcup and Surbiton written all over her. Iretha shuddered at the thought: Sidcup. About now Teresa and all the stupid bitches like her would be mincing down the High Street, all dolled up and giggly and off to meet their boyfriends for lunch somewhere. Somewhere 'grown up' —like a pub. They were too 'nice' to settle for a fumble behind the bushes in the park. They were all the same: all tarted up in their nice little jobs and itching to get married as soon as possible. OK, so Zac went off with Jake sometimes and the caravan stank and the Welsh spoke Welsh to prove some stupid point, but it wasn't so bad here. Like when they went up into the Preselis at nights and sat around on the stones, smoking joints while Zac and Jake played their guitars. That's what it was all about—being free. Sylvie and Robert went up into the Preselis sometimes. They took the kids and a picnic and were always back before dark. Silly sods. That's when the vibes were

16

at their best, after dark. That's when you got a real spiritual feeling. Like being at Stonehenge.

It was good going down the river pools as well. Zac and Jake would strip off and dive in sometimes. They said they'd bring a salmon back, but they never did. She stripped off once, but Zac got jealous when he saw Jake leering at her. Silly sod. How Zac could think she fancied Jake she didn't know. Jake was a skinny little kid. She had never liked him but he was Zac's mate and they did things together. Once she'd hinted that she didn't like having Jake hanging about and Zac got all huffy. So she'd stopped stripping off and swimming in the pools.

One night a bailiff had tried to nick them, but he couldn't prove anything. Jake kept telling everybody they'd been chased and threatened with a gun, but it wasn't like that. The bloke had got so tired of Jake yacking on about human rights and freedoms that he'd just told them all to piss off. But Jake wouldn't give up. He kept going on about how the bailiff was a symbol of oppression; how he was an agent for rich capitalist bastards in the suppression of the poor. That's when the bailiff had got angry. He went to grab Jake, but Jake ran off, fast. It was pathetic.

The bailiff did look a bit of a wally, though, all puffed up in his wellies and tweeds with Zac and Jake standing naked in front of him. It still made her giggle, thinking about it.

The old Transit van came up the track. Jake was at the wheel. He jumped out as her eyes searched for Zac.

'Where is he?'

'Zac?'

'Yeah.'

Jake shrugged and leaned into the van to drag an old army kit bag off the passenger seat. He slammed the driver's door.

'He's knocking about somewhere.'

'But where?'

She followed him to the caravan.

'With some people up at Brecon. Said he'd be back tomorrow. Got any lager, babe?'

She stepped out and reached under the caravan, pulling out a six-pack of cans. Zac kept saying he'd find an old fridge somewhere, but he'd never got round to it.

Jake wrenched at the ring pull and flung back his head as he pressed the can to his lips. His long, black, greasy hair hung down from underneath a grubby baseball cap. Iretha sat on the caravan step, in her black singlet and ragged jeans. Jake was watching her, standing over her in the caravan doorway.

'You been lonely, babe?'

She shrugged: 'I mooched around.'

He stepped over and around her, flung the empty can under the caravan and opened another.

'We'll take some up to the stones tonight, eh babe?'

She grimaced: 'Could do.'

He sauntered across the bare patch of earth which served as a yard in front of the caravan, kicked at a stone and turned.

'Zac reckons he's getting a group together.'

'Does he?' She showed the slightest spark of interest.

He sat cross-legged on the earth in front of her, swigging the lager. 'That's what he's doing—talking to people—getting things sorted.'

'How many?'

He sniffed: 'Four, five—one's got a sax.'

He drained the second can and slung it after the first. That was what Zac was always after—heading up a group. He once said that she could sing for him. She'd written a few songs already, but she hadn't told him. It was a surprise.

Jake rolled a joint and lay flat on his back on the bare earth. He pretended to shoot at a buzzard floating and crying high above them.

'Got any grub, babe?'

She got up and went into the caravan. The tops of her thighs and curve of her bottom showed through ragged slits in the back of her jeans. Jake watched appreciatively.

She opened a tin of beans and toasted a slice of bread. Outside the buzzard cried again and Jake shouted 'bang, bang'. They would get

18

some chips later, on the way to the stones. It was good, eating chips and sitting on the stones with the air full of the smell of hay.

She went out, the beans and toast on a plastic plate. Jake was dozing. She prodded him with her toe. He sat up.

'The pigs nicked me,' he announced.

'Oh yeah?'

She sat on the step and rolled a joint. Jake ate for a few moments.

'They said the tyres were shot.'

She looked at the rusting van. It was a dirty red-brown colour anyway, except for the driver's door. That was yellow. Zac had picked it up at a scrap yard when the hinges rotted off the other.

'All of them?'

The tyres didn't look that bad.

'Three. They also did me for no handbrake.'

She sniffed and drew on the joint. Jake sniffed and rubbed his mouth with a grubby hand.

'Will they be coming here?'

'Who—the pigs?'

'No, the lot Zac's with—the group.'

He shrugged: 'They might. It's Zac's scene.'

He jumped up, leaving the dirty plate on the ground, and squeezed past her to get into the caravan. Then he came out with his old guitar, sat with his back to the Transit and began strumming something by Dylan. Iretha folded her arms round her knees and stared at the Preselis. There were tractors and machinery working in the fields right up to the edge of the hills. Behind the caravan old Evans was driving his Land Rover across the field, making his sheep kick up a racket. They hadn't spoken to him since he'd shot their Lurcher. He said it was chasing his stupid ewes. Silly bugger. How could you have a dog if you didn't let it run around? Dogs had a right to freedom, just like people. Anyway, the sheep were all bunched up together on the other side of the field. The dog was nowhere near them.

She got up and ambled across to an old bit of tree trunk sticking out of the nettles which ringed the 'yard'. The wood struck warm through her jeans. Cows were trailing down the hillside from

Bryn-glas further along the lane, their udders slack and floppy. The sun was beginning to set over Cardigan Bay, shining straight into her eyes. Jake's guitar glowed a mellow chestnut in the light and the Preselis were wrapped in a misty shadow. Jake stopped playing. The sheep behind the caravan were quiet again. A blackbird or something was making a racket in the hedge along the lane. She went back to the caravan and took an old leather jacket from the seat just inside the door. Jake jumped up.

'You ready then?'

She got into the Transit while he scrabbled under the caravan to drag out more cans. The van stank of unwashed bodies, beer and stale pot. A grubby mattress filled the load area. She put her feet up on the dashboard and let her head loll back.

'Chips?' Jake asked, struggling to find reverse.

'OK.'

'Got some dough?'

'Enough.'

She thought of Teresa and the others, back in Sidcup—wrapped up in pink towelling robes after a bath and hair wash, curled up on sofas watching telly with Mum and Dad before going out. Silly bitches. She could see them—all tarted up, giggling and holding hands with naff boyfriends in naff pubs. She picked up an old newspaper from the van floor. There was a piece about extremists threatening to burn down the houses of English people who objected to their children being taught in Welsh. She told Jake about it.

'Stupid bastards,' he grunted.

'You think so?'

She wanted reassurance. It frightened her thinking that a Welshman might do something nasty to her just because she was English.

'Well, I mean . . . you know, all this global togetherness stuff and they're fucking up the system.'

'How do you mean?'

'Well, this burning business . . . It's kids' stuff, aint it? When there's the nuclear business and global warming and that.'

They sat on a stone eating chips—lukewarm, but better than

20

anything she ever cooked. Jake threw the wrappers in the van and picked up his guitar. She took off her boots and began to dance round the stones, rolling a joint. After a couple of drags, she stuffed it into the corner of Jake's mouth. It was good, dancing barefoot round the stones. The grass was soft and springy. She cupped her hands behind her head and swayed from side to side. Jake watched her. So what? Through the gathering heavy mist there came the moan of a foghorn out in the Irish Sea. It moaned again. Jake jumped up.

'Fuck this!'

He grabbed her arm and dragged her to the van.

'Jake!' she protested.

But he jumped in the Transit and turned on the engine. In the reflected light of the headlamps his face was pale and tense.

She giggled: 'You're scared, Jake,'

His face clouded: 'Shut up, you silly cow.'

He turned towards Newport instead of the caravan. She said nothing. In the town she felt him relax.

'Fancy a walk, babe?'

He was grinning now.

Down by the beach, he stuffed two fresh beer cans in the pockets of his old bomber jacket.

'How naff,' he grunted, as odds and ends of the holiday crowd mooched through the mist along the sands in holiday outfits.

Iretha said nothing. Zac was a bastard, clearing off like that. She picked up a pebble and flung it into the sea.

Back in the Transit, Jake pointed towards the common land across the bay.

'We'll go across, eh babe?'

'OK.'

She knew what he was angling at. She sat back, her feet on the dashboard but a foot or two apart this time. Sod Zac. He wasn't thinking about her, that was for sure. And Jake wasn't so bad—a bit of a kid, but he meant no harm. She cupped her hands over her crutch. Jake turned into the High Street.

'Was she up at Brecon—the red-head?'

She tried to sound casual. Only silly bitches like Teresa got up-tight when they thought their men were screwing around. Jake also attempted to sound casual, his eyes fixed on the road.

'She was about.'

Iretha said nothing. Perhaps Jake would take that hint—tit for tat, that sort of thing. As they crossed the river bridge she started to sing. Very quietly, but enough to let him know. 'Lay Lady Lay'—the Dylan song he was always singing, with his eyes on her. Poor sod; stuck out in the back of the van every night, sleeping on that grubby mattress while she and Zac humped away in the caravan.

The van lurched across the common. Jake parked behind a dune, cut the engine and switched out the lights. It seemed stupid, but it was better than being alone in the caravan again. She climbed into the back. Jake followed. Sod Zac.

Jake messed it all up because he was a kid really and couldn't control himself. They lay on their backs and smoked a joint. The van's roof was damp with condensation.

'You in the group?'

Jake drew on the joint.

'Yeah—on bass.'

Silence, the atmosphere now thick with the sweet smell of pot.

'He said you could sing if you want.'

'I might.'

She leant over to take the joint. The zip of her jacket rubbed against her nipple. Zac didn't like her tits. He said they were too small. He was a jerk really: like all men, hung up on big tits and neat bums. It was time to jack him in. Bugger his group, she would stay in the caravan. At twenty she was old enough to do as she pleased. After all, that's what she'd come here for—to be free of hassle.

The Bakery

Arthur Elias liked to remember the village in its heyday, when the pit-head and tips loomed over the hap-hazard rows of miners' terraces, bleak, black and seemingly indomitable. In those days, six pubs met the needs of shift-thirsty colliers, fifteen shops the requirements of their wives and, on high days and holidays, George Crundle would clean up his coaches to carry flocks of families off to the beach—to Aberavon, Mumbles or even Tenby. Between times, George's buses ran back and forth along the valley sides, to and from Swansea and running the gamut with Geoff Hawkins's coal lorries on the narrow, twisting road.

Geoff's coal yard lay apart from the pit, of course: the daily discharges from there went off down the valley in black and battered railway trucks, but the fortunes of Geoff's fifteen workers were as integral to the pit as those of the men who hewed the coal.

Elsewhere, three petrol stations and a couple of garages kept the cars of the village mobile, the Co-op Funeral Parlour laid out the community's dead to rest, the Chapel was rarely less than three parts full and, on Tuesdays and Thursdays, two women came up the valley on a Crundle bus to open up the library from ten o'clock to four.

Then the pit closed, and it all went—bit by bit. Sally Morgan put up the shutters at her little haberdashery; bus by bus and coach by coach, the Crundle fleet diminished. Geoff Hawkins cast around for other loads, but there were none, and in the very week that boards were nailed over the windows of the Avon Arms, the Co-op closed the funeral parlour. Soon after, Alan Jones packed up selling petrol.

Now, Arthur reflected, just two pubs and one petrol station remained. Stan Jones still sold his meat, Billy Davies his magazines, newspapers, sweets and tobacco and Dyfrig Williams his bread and cakes. Frattoni's fish and chips was hanging on, while Betty Saunders's general store was one of those mini-market places—eight-to-eight and open Sundays.

23

It was Billy who broke the news about Dyfrig when he and Arthur sat down for a pint at the Mason's.

'He's packing up, is Dyfrig—told me this morning.'

Billy was pink and white and dapper, and a little excited by the news.

'Never!'

Arthur, lean, lined, dark and rheumatic from years down the pit, eyed his companion with disbelief over the rim of his glass.

'That's what he said,' Billy chirped. 'Packing up this spring, he reckons.'

Arthur manipulated an aching knee. There was a time, he reflected, when Billy and his shop were as grimy with coal dust as the rest of them.

'I doubt the boy will take it on then?'

Billy wrinkled his nose: 'A place like that, mun, with the job he's got?'

Billy was right. Arthur remembered Annie telling him, when she taught at the school and shared his love of poetry, that Dyfrig's boy was one of the brightest she'd known. And she was right: a degree in economics and then the Civil Service. And the girls had done well, mind: Elizabeth married to a BBC producer and Geraldine teaching French at a Cardiff comprehensive. The three of them still spoke Welsh, but it was the Welsh of the middle-class, S4C age, not of the village in which they grew up.

'The truth is, Arthur,' Billy confided, with an almost delicate sip of his beer, 'Dyfrig's kids have done too well for a place like this. Anyway, what would they get out of it? It'd cost them a fortune to put the place right—with loans and the like.'

Billy knew he was right: Billy liked to face facts. Being a business-man, he understood the Thatcherite catchphrase of 'market forces'. At least, that was how he saw things when it came to survival in business. Arthur suspected it saved him from thinking about life on a broader, deeper plane, and from the realisation that had he been a tailor, he would have been out of business long ago.

But Billy was right in part about the bakery. It was well known that Dyfrig's ability to escape the clutches of the Council's environmental

24

health people depended entirely on Councillor Tom Harries being his brother-in-law.

Billy was onto another track.

'See, Arthur, people these days want their bread wrapped and tidy. Look at that pair in the mini-market—I bet they sell more wrapped bread in a day than Dyfrig does in three, and it's all from a properly set up factory. That's the way it is, mun—you can't escape the facts.'

Arthur could find no answer. He took a well-used tin from the pocket of his well-used jacket and rolled a cigarette. Billy was the one who did the talking whenever the pair got together. He was doing so now.

'See, I've always said, mun, that the best thing for youngsters around here is to get themselves educated and get out. Look at Stan's grandson, now: are you saying he'll be best off coming back from that Polytechnic or whatever to chop up bits of brisket for you and pieces of scrag end for old Sally—course you can't!'

'But they don't all go to university and the like,' Arthur pointed out with mournful adroitness.

'I'm not saying that, mun, but with their cars and motorbikes and a bit of education, why stay here when they can go off down Swansea and get a job on computers at the car licencing place?' Billy slapped his knee, as if to stress the absolute truth of his argument. 'I would have done, Arthur—after the war. If you'd have given me a bit of cash and an old motorbike, I'd have been off. Only marrying stopped me.'

Arthur's thoughts went back to his days in the pit: to nights at the now-closed Welfare Hall, to the singing in the pubs, the Eisteddfodau in every valley village, the Workers Education Association night classes.

True, he had once wished for a better education, so he had attended those classes and had read avidly, buying books on the never-never, borrowing from the library. He was lucky, being married to a teacher. But was chasing after an education and a good career really the answer? It did nothing for the communities the brightest youngsters left behind: they just created an intellectual

25

vacuum. He cold not find the words to argue this with Billy. Billy would never understand what an informal, self-education had given Arthur. It was a sense of deep fulfilment, which had nothing to do with his status as a coal-face worker; nothing to do with a burning desire to escape the village and earn high wages in an office. Of course you didn't need a degree to run a bakery, he wanted to tell Billy. It would just be nice to have somebody there who could offer the community more than loaves of white bread, fancy cakes and fruit pies. There was more to the decline of the community than the loss of the pithead.

Billy's assumption that Dyfrig was closing down the bakery for good received a bit of a jolt when Dyfrig himself announced he had sold the place. The mild pleasure gained from this news was offset by the intelligence that the buyers came from Portsmouth. Up in one of the new houses on the Mountain Road, Tomos Thomas began writing letters to the District Council planning department demanding that the place be taken over by a Welsh buyer. A bemused director of planning pointed out that he had no control or jurisdiction over the sale of businesses and private property. Tomos Thomas was not satisfied and cast around for more support.

According to Dyfrig, his buyer was a bakery salesman for a big factory, while his wife did catering work. Billy was perplexed.

'Can't see it makes sense, myself,' he told Arthur, as they settled at a table in the Masons. 'Him giving up a job like that to take on Dyfrig's place. Anyroad, what does a man like that know about baking decent bread? And where's the call for her catering work?'

Billy took a sip of his beer, satisfied his original prognosis for the bakery would surely prove correct.

Arthur lit a rumpled cigarette for the second time, and stretched out an aching leg. He would not admit as much to Billy, but there was little call for catering in the village these days. He remembered the days when Dyfrig was up at three in the morning, baking for a wedding. He would turn out little rolls and loaves of bread by the dozen and the women would come down and collect them up and take them home to fill the rolls and make sandwiches. They would decorate Dyfrig's little buns themselves, just to keep the costs down.

In those days, the wedding parties walked down the streets from the Chapel to the Welfare Hall, a pub or just the bride's house to enjoy the food provided by the women.

Now they drove off down the valley to big hotels in Swansea, where girls in white blouses and boys in bow ties fussed over bits and pieces of food laid out on buffet tables. And all the youngsters thought it wonderful, and very posh.

Even so, Arthur would have liked to challenge Billy's blithe assumption.

'So you don't think there's much in it for the bakery, then?'

'No: can't see a couple like that make a go of it. As I said, it'll cost 'em a fortune to put right for a start.'

On his own with Dyfrig in the shop the following morning, Arthur decided to test Billy's thesis on the bakery, slipping the subject into their conversation as he bought a small white loaf, two bath buns and little fruit cake. With Annie dead these past ten years, he bought little and often. That way he got out of the house more frequently: kept himself in touch with those around him.

'So when will you be gone then?'

Dyfrig brushed crumbs from the counter. He was lean and grey, his hands soft and white, his apron a little grimy.

'June, I reckon.'

'Can you see them lasting?'

Dyfrig shrugged, leaning on the counter to bring himself closer to Arthur, thus implying a measure of confidentiality.

'The thing is, Arthur, I got my price so what they do is their business. They've been thorough, mind.' He straightened up and brushed a hand across the counter again. 'Aye, they've been through the books, brought in an accountant, got a list of every hotel, pub, cafe, guest-house, restaurant and bed and breakfast place in the area . . . even wanted to know how many people worked on that little industrial estate down at Drefach.'

Arthur looked suitably impressed. Dyfrig began fussing over a selection of cakes in a glass display case.

'So it's up to them, Arthur. They know the score—even been to the environmental health people,' he added, with a wink. He leaned on the counter again. 'As for me, I've got my little bungalow lined up and I'm ready to go.'

'Where're you off to, then?'

Arthur had in mind a place on the Mountain Road—one with a new 'sold' sign in the garden.

'Tenby!' Dyfrig beamed across the counter. 'Remember, Arthur; George and his coaches and half the village on the beach? Well, I've always said, if I had the money, that's where I'd go. That's how we got together, see? The Missus and me. Damn there was a fuss! Got behind a sand dune and missed the bus home, we did.'

He laughed with a newly-fresh pleasure at the memory, and Arthur saw in the laughter a man relieved at last to be free not just from his business but the community.

'You'll not miss it, then?'

Dyfrig grinned. 'Miss it? Damn, man, if I could have sold this place years ago, I would have gone like a shot.' He imitated the swing of a golfer teeing off. 'Aye, from now on it's golf for me.'

Arthur wondered how a man could show so much delight in getting away from the community. But then Dyfrig was always a bit of an odd one out, what with his early starts in the bakery, long days in the shop and early nights. Nor was he much of a reader. But then, like Billy, he was a shopkeeper. They weren't like pit men—they lacked the comradeship, the common bond.

When Arthur woke he noticed the breeze was free of the aroma of baking bread. He was reminded of the first morning after the pit closed. Then it was the silence that hit him: the lack of clamour as men changed shifts, shouting greetings, banging doors and revving engines outside Billy's shop, all against a backdrop of clamour from the pit—the hooters, winding gear and crash of coal dropped from large grabs into the bodies of rail trucks.

The silence that morning had un-nerved Arthur for a while, just as the clear, fresh breeze which blew in through his window did now. He felt at something of a loss without that re-assuring smell of bread drifting up the hill towards him. He eased a rheumatic leg

28

off the bed and dressed, in melancholy mood. No doubt Dyfrig was rushing about, packing his bags and anxious to be off.

As a handful of middle-aged and elderly people straggled away from the Chapel the following evening, the new owners of the bakery arrived. Early on the Monday they took delivery of bread and cakes baked in a factory down in Swansea, and the shop opened as usual. From out the back there came the sound of men dismantling Dyfrig's old equipment.

The man was thick-set, dark-haired and cheerful, about middle-height and middle-aged and keen to know his customers. She was a little on the plump side, mousey-haired and less forthcoming. There were no children and neither appeared to be the lean, keen executive type of recent local imagination.

For two weeks the bakery was in turmoil: the old equipment was ripped out, builders moved in and fitters arrived to set up the new ovens. As promised by Wyatt, the new owner, the bakery fired up again within a fortnight, and Arthur woke up once again to the smell of new bread drifting through his window. Two men setting off for an early shift in Swansea saw Wyatt pull out of the bakery yard in a small van loaded to the roof. By nine o'clock he was back again, to help his wife in the shop.

In less than a month, Debbie—who used to work for Dyfrig—was out and about in a second van, while Eluned Hughes and young John Watson worked in the bakery. During the afternoons, his sister came in to give Jenny Wyatt a break from the shop.

Billy was unmoved.

'Can't see it lasting myself,' he declared to Arthur at the Masons. 'Trade's good for now, maybe, but for how long? The novelty will wear off man, you'll see.'

Arthur smiled to himself and rolled a cigarette. Billy was piqued. He was being shown up. While he and the likes of Dyfrig just did what had to be done and dreamed of escape, the Wyatts were applying a bit of enthusiasm and dedication to their business.

Debbie was the first to put the word out that there was more to the bakery couple than met the eye. They were both graduates, she let slip—he in engineering, she in physics.

'Funny that,' Billy mused, a blob of froth from his fresh pint framing his upper lip. 'You wouldn't think, with degrees like that, they'd be throwing it all away on a bit of a bakery. What's engineering got to do with baking bread, eh? Or physics?'

Arthur rubbed his thigh and remained silent, contenting himself with a glow of private satisfaction. Billy persisted.

'I mean, it doesn't seem right, does it? Them throwing all that education away and hiding away down here. You'd think they were running away from something.'

Arthur leaned forward, picked up his glass, took a sip and returned to mug to the table.

'You know, Billy,' he announced quietly, 'I've never thought education was all about smart jobs and clean fingernails.'

Billy opened and closed his mouth, lost for words.

'It's been too much of an excuse for us, you know,' Arthur persisted, staring at his pint pot and rubbing his knee. 'Too much of an excuse for running away. Damn man, there are better read men down the pits than half your fancy graduates . . .' He raised a hand to staunch an interjection, 'and what they learned was respect for themselves as men. You never did come up the reading room, did you, boy? Never heard them talking and arguing?'

They were silent for a moment. For once Arthur held the floor. He re-lit his cigarette.

'Aye,' he pondered. 'You remember little Nest, don't you?'

Billy looked wary, and nodded.

Nest was Arthur's only child who went off to Cardiff to study nursing. At the age of twenty-two she came off the back of her boyfriend's motorbike and never re-gained consciousness.

'Well,' said Arthur, 'she said once she wanted to come back here and I said why not—she would have to travel to Swansea to work, mind. And she said no, it was no use: there wasn't the intellectual stimulation she needed. All the youngsters like her with a bit of life and imagination in them had gone away—like she had. With the Welfare Hall and reading room gone, what was there to do—except drink?'

Billy looked dumbfounded: 'Are you sayin', Arthur, that little

Nest and the likes of her should have stayed here and worked with me and Dyfrig and the like—or gone down the pit?'

Arthur glanced around the bar room. It was all but empty again—just a handful of men whiling away their empty evening hours. Once the place was packed with men arguing and debating and, at the end of the evening, singing.

'Why not?' he challenged Billy. 'One time brains as good as theirs, or better, had no choice. Before the '44 Education Act it was out of school and down the pit—even after. And it was people like them who kept the place going.'

Billy leaned forward, resting an arm on the table.

'But you can't hold people back, Arthur—it's not right.'

Arthur shifted his leg and winced.

'I know that man, but what I'm saying is this: remember how Tomos Thomas and the like said the bakery shouldn't be going to an English couple?'

'Aye.'

'Well, it struck me then and not for the first time, we're too damned keen on paper qualifications to see a good day's work when it needs to be done. Who made the fuss, eh? That Thomas bloke and the likes of him in the smart houses up on the Mountain Road with their smart jobs in Swansea. All educated, see? And all thinking they're too good for baking. Even Dyfrig's Elizabeth said he should've found a local buyer. But has she and her TV husband come back to take over? 'Course not!'

Billy swallowed and blinked.

'But damn it, man . . .' he began to protest. Arthur raised a hand to silence him, and reached for matches in his old jacket.

'What I'm saying, boy, is this: education isn't about running away to take up smart little jobs—it's about knowing you're happy; knowing you're content to be what you are. That's what the Wyatts are telling us, boy—and damn good luck to them.'

31

The Search

'Our chances of success would have been much improved had you called us earlier, Mrs James.'

With that, Chief Inspector Andrew Browning settled on an upright, metal-framed chair and crossed his long legs. He was clearly annoyed at being called out to search for an elderly woman in the lowering light of a cold December afternoon.

'I am sorry, Chief Inspector, but it was only by chance that we discovered Miss Griffiths would not be back at her usual time.'

Janet James skilfully turned apology into rebuke with the practised ease of one well-accustomed to dealing with the peevish and obdurate.

Browning remained cool: 'By what chance was that, may I ask?'

Beneath the urbanity he was ill at ease: successful, ambitious women un-nerved him and Janet James, Medical Services Manager for the Victoria Physchiatric Hospital in Merthyr Dewi, was clearly one such. He uncrossed his thighs and rested his elbows on his knees. A graduate in physical education from Loughborough University, his gaunt face and balding scalp conjured the image of an Oxford don in uniform. In contrast, Janet James was short, dark and determined. She settled back into her imposing leather chair, her soft, rounded features tense with anxiety under a halo of black curls. If she was thirty five, then Browning was ten years older.

'Miss Griffiths normally goes into town immediately afer lunch,' Janet James began to explain. 'She goes to the market cafe, gossips with anyone who will chat to her and returns by 3.30. However, twenty minutes ago we received a call from a local bus company to say one of its drivers had taken a fare from an elderly woman who wished to go to Tregwynt. Instead, she alighted at Llanarth. When the driver remarked on this, she appeared flustered and said something about getting back to the Hospital. Unfortunately she was already off the bus, and hurried away. The driver immediately 'phoned his depot, and they 'phoned us.'

'And this was at what time?'

Browning wished he was working in a large city station, with the ever present opportunities for promotion and more to occupy him than missing women. Somehow his ambitions had gone completely awry since the incident with Jennifer.

'At 3.15—I checked.'

Janet James was clearly on top of her job.

'And did somebody go to look for Miss Griffiths?'

'Staff Nurse Moses went immediately. He 'phoned just before you arrived to say he had found nothing.'

'And is he still there?'

'Yes.'

'Then I will send some men to him immediately and launch a search.'

'Thank you, Chief Inspector.'

Janet James managed to imply that that was the least she expected.

Radios crackled and orders were issued. Policemen, dogs and vehicles came and went in the dark of the Hospital car park. Blue lights flashed and headlamps shone. Janet James, in her office over-looking the scene, ordered cups of tea as Browning returned to establish a constant surveillence over his men outside.

'How . . .' He paused for a moment, leaning against the window frame and unsure as to whether he should use the word 'ill' in relation to Miss Griffiths's state of mind.

'Disturbed is the appropriate word, Chief Inspector,' Janet James interjected. 'Within the Hospital and with her daily trips to town, she can cope. Beyond that she becomes confused and anxious.'

'Then she is not ill as such?'

'No Chief Inspector, she was never ill.'

Browning turned from the window and sat again on the hard chair.

'But how?'

Beyond the car park activity, lights shone out from all parts of the great Victorian hospital block. Janet James's office was situated in the former overseer's house, from which a reign of terror and

33

brutality was once exercised over patients and staff alike. She drew in a deep breath.

'We must go back to 1928, Chief Inspector, when Megan Griffiths was a girl of 16.'

Yet even Janet James did not know the full extent of Megan Griffiths's story.

*   *   *

Megan Griffiths was the daughter of a modestly successful, God-fearing, chapel-going farmer who assumed that, on leaving school at the age of thirteen, his daughter would remain at home until she found a suitable husband: a young man of similar background, social status and religious belief. Until he arrived on the scene, Megan's time at home would be considered an apprenticeship for her future domestic responsibilities. She was too high up on the social scale to go out to work, too low down to be considered worthy of any further education. So she would learn to cook and clean and care for the home under the wing of her mother.

This was taken for granted, as was one other thing: Megan would be taught nothing about sex. As a physically-advanced fifteen-year-old, she even wondered if periods afflicted all girls, for in those days girls rarely began menstruation before they left school. So, denied the reassurance of shared experiences with school-day companions, Megan became convinced she was unique among her contemporaries. All the more so, because her body was more that of a woman than a young girl and this she found embarrassing and confusing.

For the boys in the village, there was nothing embarrassing or confusing about the burgeoning figure of Megan Griffiths, and such was their desire to gain closer aquaintance that she positively sought refuge among her girlfriends whenever teenagers of both sexes were allowed to meet. The boys, she sensed, showed an interest which had nothing to do with her growing skills in the art of being a good, conscientious wife.

Yet, while distancing herself from the attentions of the local boys, Megan Griffiths grew increasingly curious and troubled in her lone

34

search for an explanation as to why she created so much interest. She decided to seek help, but being the eldest in her family, she could not turn to an elder sister or sympathetic sister-in-law. She turned, instead, to someone she felt she could trust implicitly: a person who would not talk out of turn and would at all times honour the confidentiality of their discussions.

*   *   *

Browning shuddered inwardly as Janet James re-called the tale with what little detail she had to hand. He was thinking of a newly-promoted, red-haired sergeant called Jennifer. She, like him, was a Chief Inspector now. He was told she lived in a docklands flat and drove a white Volkswagen Golf convertible. She was where he had hoped to be. He forced his mind back to Miss Griffiths.

'So she has been a patient for sixty years?'

'Precisely.'

His radio crackled: blue lights continued to blink in the car park. For sixty years Megan Griffiths had been condemned to this awful place for giving birth to an illegitimate child. Jennifer had taken an afternoon's leave to abort his child, and had returned the next day as if nothing had happened. Pregnancy to Jennifer had been nothing more than an inconvenient hiccup on her route to greater success. He had wanted the child: had wanted to be its true and proper father. Browning took a deep breath.

'So what happened to the child?' he asked quietly.

Janet James shrugged: 'There's no record. Apparently Miss Griffiths used to go round saying "they took it away—the baby went," but that was drummed out of her. Remember, Chief Inspector, she was deemed a "moral degenerate" and was therefore condemned "mad" and "evil". She had to be punished.'

'And the father?'

'Who knows, except for Miss Griffiths—and him. Again, she used to say "he was a good man, not an evil one," but that was also drummed out of her. She was forced to make her every action, every word, a denial of the truth.'

35

Browning stood and returned to the window.

'You are a nurse, Mrs James?'

She swung round in her chair and looked up at the lanky, uniformed frame and smiled.

'Yes. Twenty years ago I would have been the matron. Now I sit at a computer, juggling staff-patient ratios, bed-space usage and the cost-effectiveness of staffing levels.'

Browning's radio crackled and he was called away. On his return, Janet James was anxious for news.

'Nothing, I'm afraid.'

He looked distracted—as if his mind was on other things.

'Tell me, Mrs James, was there anything unusual about Miss Griffiths's behaviour today?'

He recalled how Jennifer sometimes became moody and distracted. He wondered if she regretted the abortion and one day dared to ask. Her response was hostile and angry. He was left puzzled and hurt. Eventually, tired of the strain of working close to Jennifer, he had opted for a transfer to Merthyr Dewi.

Janet James was explaining how Megan Griffiths had been anxious to have her mid-morning drink earlier than usual—and her lunch, 'but sometimes patients do get confused with the time,' the nurse-administrator concluded.

'I see.'

A sergeant knocked on the door and entered the office. A constable on house-to-house enquiries had reported in. He had spoken to a Mr Thomas of Bro Eynon, Llanddewi who was 'very jumpy'.

'Apparently Thomas said the woman was a moral degenerate who had brought shame on a man honoured in the eyes of God, Sir.'

Browning frowned and thought for a moment. Thomas clearly knew more than he admitted. It would be interesting to talk to him.

'Leave it for the moment, Sergeant: Miss Griffiths comes first.'

Megan Griffiths was found dead from exposure in a ditch in the fields between Llanarth and Tregwynt, her thin, ill-fitting raincoat covered in glistening frost. How she came to be there, no one could be sure. It was suspected she had strayed from a long-disused

36

footpath which once linked the two villages: a path she would have known well in her youth.

After a night of worry and waiting, a hollow-eyed Janet James prepared herself for the meetings, discussions and paperwork which inevitably followed the death of a patient in unusual circumstances. Browning, equally grey and hollow-eyed, left her office and stepped out into the car park. In the pale, cool sunlight of a December morning he found himself suddenly longing to talk to Jennifer, and he knew why. He wanted to tell her, with malicious delight, how lucky she had been; to scrape away at her conscience for any signs of regret or remorse. He wanted . . . but he knew it would be of no use.

He sat in the back of his car, his driver awaiting orders. She was a constable—a local girl.

'An awful thing, Davies—to be shut away; to be called mad and evil, just for having a baby.'

The girl shrugged: 'It was like that around here once, sir. There used to be dozens like Miss Griffiths in the old Victoria.'

'But how . . .?'

Browning gave up. If he were to understand more about the life of Megan Griffiths, he suspected he would need to talk to Mr Thomas.

The old man was a stocky, bow-legged character, with a square, double-chinned face criss-crossed with the blue and red veins of a lifetime exposed to the elements. He appeared at the door of his council house in an aged three-piece suit and collarless white shirt. Grudgingly, he ushered Browning into a front room furnished in a style befitting a period long before the place was built.

Settling into a worn, wing chair beside a fireplace filled by a Parkray boiler, Thomas listened with care as Browning repeated the old man's comments to the constable.

'That's all I can say, sir,' Thomas declared, lifting his chin to stress the finality of his words.

Browning persisted, quietly and gently, taking a chance that Thomas knew nothing of inquests.

'We will need to know precisely the state of mind in which Miss Griffiths found herself on the day she died, Mr Thomas.'

The old man raised an eyebrow in surprise at Browning's particular choice of words.

'I would have thought, Sir, her state of mind was well known. Should have been, anyroad. See, as I told that Constable of yours, I last saw that Megan sixty years back after Chapel one Sunday—and that's the sum of it.'

Browning's knees were all but level with his chest where he sat on the shabby, sunken sofa. A clock ticked on the mantelpiece, flanked by silver-framed photographs, one or two of them—he guessed—dating from the days when the scandal of Megan Griffiths held the neighbourhood in thrall.

'Did you know about the baby?'

Thomas rubbed a grey-stubbled chin and look discomforted.

'Not exactly—not then. I was just a youngster, see? But gossip always travels. Aye . . .'

He gazed at the red glow behind the glass fire door.

'Gossip about the father, perhaps?'

Thomas looked briefly startled. Browning continued, his voice quiet in the warm, heavily-furnished room.

'A name or names must have been mentioned, surely?'

Thomas scratched his forehead: 'Aye, and some too daft to mention.'

'Why?'

Thomas sniffed and stared directly at Browning.

'Because it was wrong, sir, what was said—it was a slander.'

Browning shifted his position, leaning his knees to one side. On the low sofa he felt inferior to Thomas, but he knew that if he stood his tall frame would dominate the old man.

'You said "a man honoured in the eyes of God." A minister, perhaps?'

Thomas shot Browning a quick, fearful glance and rubbed his eyes.

'It was as I said, sir.'

'A Minister, then.'

Thomas sighed and stared at the fire.

'Aye, sir—but not the one they said him to be.'

Browning waited, sensing the old man was ready to talk. Thomas rubbed a rough hand over his rough chin.

'See sir, when Megan got herself into trouble, there was all sorts to pay. Nothing was said in simple words, mind. Megan just went off and the next Sunday the Ministers were up in their pulpits stormin' on about the sins of the flesh and the wickedness of temptresses. Ours said somethin' about fornication. I puzzled about that for days —I were only thirteen then. Anyroad, we guessed it were all to do with Megan. 'Course, we boys still couldn't be sure what it was about exactly, but when someone said Williams, the Minister at Tregwynt was involved also, we had a good guess.'

'So Williams was the one that was slandered, Mr Thomas.'

'Aye, sir.'

After the abortion the tension between Browning and Jennifer had reached a point whereby they could not work the same shift together. Knowing Jennifer would not budge, Browning had applied for and been granted his transfer to Merthyr Dewi. Afterwards the tale went round that he had been made to go, as a subtle punishment for his sexist arrogance towards a female officer of equal rank; that he was jealous of Jennifer's success and potential for promotion, that she had laid a complaint against him. At least he had managed to keep pace with her, rank for rank.

'So who was the Minister, Mr Thomas?'

The old man stared at the fire, grudging in his admission.

'It were Pritchard, here at Llanddewi, Sir. He was young then— new to the Ministry—but he stayed on till he finished. He bought himself a cottage just down the road when he did. Anyways, he was always a lonely sort—kept himself to himself, but when he took bad I thought only neighbourly to see him in Hospital.' Thomas turned his face towards Browning: 'That's when he began talking, see?'

Browning linked long fingers round his knees and leaned forward. 'And . . .?'

Thomas hesitated: 'Well, the thing was . . . It seems Megan came to him and said she didn't like it, the way boys stared at her and the like. She got right upset and started crying, so he put her arms round her—just for a bit of comfort, see? Well, that were it, what with the two of them on their own in the Manse, like. When the baby started, Pritchard reckoned he panicked—rushed off to Williams, who had her put away.'

'And no question of marriage . . .'

Browning was treated to a humourless smile.

'She were young, sir, and anyroad, the Griffithses were Baptists, Pritchard a Calvinist.'

'Did he ever see her, after that?'

Thomas frowned: 'I doubt it, sir—but there were a tale at one time that a man wrote to her every week or suchlike. He never signed a name or gave an address, just said he prayed for her and begged her forgiveness.'

'Pritchard?'

'It seems like, sir.'

'And what happened to the baby?'

Thomas scratched the top of his head: 'Who's to say, sir, who's to say . . .'

Jennifer had fixed the abortion before telling Browning she was pregnant. He wanted to run now from the stuffy, over-furnished room and tell her all he had been told. He wanted to watch as her determination that she was entirely right crumbled into tears of remorse; to see her face lined with sorrow and regret. But it was no use. Megan was from a past for which Jennifer had no time. She lived for the present and the future.

Browning took a deep breath: 'When did Mr Pritchard tell you this, Mr Thomas?'

'Yesterday, sir—at the Merthyr General.'

'And is he very ill?'

Thomas sighed and stared at the fire and scratched his chin. Then in a voice which said he had said enough, he announced: 'He's dead, sir—died last night, he did.'

A Bit of Fun

I'm tellin' you now, boys—the police aren't interested. It's time we did somethin' for ourselves.'

Robert leaned across the small, round table, tense and intense, a heavy lock of black hair falling across his forehead, partially masking horn-rimmed glasses. Burly, slope-shouldered and given to wearing baggy, hand-knitted sweaters, he eyed his drinking companions carefully: Emrys, slim, blond and trim; Meurig, tall, dark and sanguine, and Matt. Matt, medium height, medium build and mousey haired, looked jumpy.

'Like what?' he blurted out, eyeing his mates anxiously with nervous brown eyes.

Robert leaned back, brushing away the floppy lock with contrived nonchalance.

'We'll go down there, mun—go down and tell 'em straight about the boy.'

He reached for his pint, and took a swig as if to emphasise the simplicity of his idea. Only Meurig noted the slight shake of Robert's hand. He rested an ankle on a knee and leaned back on his chair.

'Tell them what?' he asked of Robert with casual disinterest.

'That the boy's a bloody nuisance, mun. We'll tell 'em we know the tricks he's up to and that we'll sort the little bugger out if the police won't.'

Meurig's face carried the hint of a smile. Matt looked both horrified and terrified. Emrys, with an ankle on a knee like Meurig, studied the sole of a grimy trainer.

'You, you, you can't do that!' Matt stammered. 'You can't go bargin' in on them like that. You've no proof.'

Robert prodded the beer-splashed table with a stubby fore-finger.

'Aye, mun, an' that's why the police have done nothin'. Say they've no proof. But we know better. Are you tellin' me the boy hasn't been round just about every place in the village, nickin' things?' He began counting off incidents on his fingers. 'Geoff's coat goes from his outhouse and two days later the boy's wanderin' round in one just like it. A radio goes from Garreg-lwyd and the next day the boy's tryin' to flog one like it at school. Money goes from Y Glyn an' next thing the boy's got a new bike. An' the bloody police say they've got no proof!'

Emrys removed his ankle from his knee and leaned forward.

'Look, man, I'm not saying we don't have our suspicions, but you can't go knocking on their door and telling his Dad he's a thief. Seems to me we'd best just give 'em a warning: enough to show we know.'

Robert glanced at Meurig and Matt. The former gave a brief nod of agreement, the latter looked happier. Robert was not to be mollified. Pushing his pint pot to the centre of the table, he leaned on the surface with his elbows.

'The way I see it, boys, is this. It's English law and the police are controlled by it. Now then, we had our own ways once—did thin's our own ways, see? An' it worked. We didn't 'ave to rely on police ten miles away to tell us what's goin' on under our noses. No proof! One time, people handled thin's the way it was best for them. English law be damned!'

Robert sat back. His expression challenged the others to contradict him. He, and perhaps his listeners too, seemed unaware that, prior to the formation of a national police force and even further back than that, communities handled the bringing of justice to miscreants in similar fashion the world over: only the punishments meted showed significant variation. Seeing political opportunity, Robert instinctively sought to play on the ignorance and emotions of the others, moulding his arguments like one well-practised in the art.

Meurig looked thoughtful and leaned forward, elbows on knees.

'Look, mun, we've no real proof. As the police say, there's nothin' to show the boy's to blame . . .'

'Damn it man!' Robert interrupted. Meurig was cool and calm—and too damned reasonable. 'What else do we do then, eh? Let the boy go on thieving?'

Meurig shook his head: 'No, no. We've just got to warn them, right? It's no place of ours to go around accusing without proof, so

42

we go there one evening, knock on the door and tell Drake we have our suspicions—just let him know we're onto the kid.'

Robert was indignant: 'We'll get nowhere like that, mun! Direct action—that's what's needed. We've got to tell 'em we're fed up with bein' messed about by the police and that we have our rights —rights that go back well before the English started pushin' us about.'

Meurig was unabashed: 'That's as maybe, but step out of line with the Drake boy, and I'll not be there beside you—understand?'

With that he sat back, hoisting his ankle back onto his knee. Robert glanced at Matt and Emrys, and knew they agreed with Meurig.

'All right, then, we'll go down there an' warn them.'

'Just us?' Matt almost squeaked in horror.

Robert smiled, glad to regain the initiative; pleased to divulge his grand plan—the plan which would make him a leader of the people.

'No, mun, the whole village! We'll put the word round, see? No fuss mind, just a whisper here, whisper there an' when everyone's outside the Drake place, we'll go up an' give Drake the warnin'.'

Meurig's smile was inscrutable, Matt looked relieved. Emrys reached for his beer mug without comment.

As they argued, Drake was drinking at The Barleycorn, on the 'A' road two miles from the village. He preferred drinking there. It was more anonymous: people came and went—people travelling past or out for an evening from the town. He could pronounce the name, as well. At the Tafarn-y-Bugail, down in the village, they were a clannish bunch. He often suspected they spoke Welsh just to exclude him. He said as much to Charlotte, once—the English girl behind the bar. She never said she was married to Robert's cousin, but that was how word of Drake's opinion got back to the ears of Llanbedr—ran along the main street and trickled down the side roads.

The village was hardly that at all: a school, pub, run-down garage and post-office cum shop straggled along a 'B' road with a handful of houses and a scattering of bungalows in between. Drake, whose fourteen-year-old son was accused of several recent thefts, lived in one of the houses: a bay-windowed detached place dating from the thirties and standing opposite the garage.

It was said Drake planned to build a bungalow in the garden. Sally Evans and her husband were furious: if the bungalow ever came about, it would overlook their back door and butt right up to their garden fence.

Tom Davies was not happy with Drake for other reasons. He had planned to buy the house ready for his retirement from the farm. He had been hanging on to get the price down a bit when Drake came along and paid every penny asked for, in cash.

At the pub, Griff recalled how his uncle grew prize vegetables where Drake's discarded Talbot Alpine now lay among nettles. The defunct car was no worry to Alan Thomas: he had half a dozen lying around the garage. His grouse was that Drake did vehicle repairs for other people, right on his business doorstep.

Drake was also unpopular with Betsan Harries at the school. Having deposited his two younger children into her educational safe-keeping, he complained continually about their lack of progress. What else did he expect? she would ask: it was a Welsh-speaking school, and did he and his wife come to chat to her about it before buying the house? Of course not!

Little was known about the Drake family. It was said he once ran a shop in Birmingham—a sports shop, or something. His wife was pleasant enough, but kept herself to herself. Drake was not nasty mind, people would add, although his eldest boy . . .

County Councillor T.H.E. Roscoe was well aware that the boy was becoming a tearaway when he straightened his tie and brushed a fleck of lint from his jacket before ringing Robert's door bell. The bungalow was modern and featureless, the front-room clinically furnished, save for an untidy desk in one corner, against which was stacked a pile of magazines and newspapers.

'Weather's holding up, then,' Roscoe observed as he hitched up his trouser legs before sitting down.

'Stayed good for the harvest, I must say.'

Whiskies were served and the small talk hung heavy in the air until

Roscoe offered up an apparently innocent speculation as to Plaid Cymru's chances of success in the next election.

'Bound to get back in round here,' Robert assured him.

'You think so?' Roscoe considered the point for a moment. Dapper and well-tailored, he was content to be sixty and successful in both his business and public life. 'Mind, a lot could happen between now and the next election.'

'Can't see so myself.' Robert, slumped in a chair, sipped his whiskey, and knew what Roscoe was getting at. 'Not the way the Conservatives are going, any road,' he added.

Each stared at the unlit gas fire.

'I was thinking of things locally, boy. You know the way it is with some of the hotheads. One silly trick and away go our chances.'

Robert re-filled the glasses.

'Things have been quiet, mind, this past year or two. Three years since the last firing, an' most people know that's not Plaid's game.'

'Damn stupid trick that,' Roscoe agreed, 'firing holiday homes.' He scratched his forehead and then looked directly at Robert. 'It was other things I was thinking about—things which could prove just as damaging.'

'Oh aye, Teg?'

Robert affected a sudden interest in a previously unheard whisper.

Roscoe crossed his legs: 'I thought you might have heard boy— about the Drake boy. The word is tomorrow night some people are going down to issue a warning or something about the thieving.'

'Is that so, Teg? Mind, the boy's a bloody nuisance—you ask anyone hereabouts.'

'Oh I know, I know.' Roscoe adopted the tone of one weighed down by civic duty. 'I had a word about him myself yesterday with the directors of education and social services. Even had a quiet word with the Chief Constable. And something is being done. I can't say exactly what, mind—but it is.'

'That so Teg?'

Roscoe sat forward: 'Of course it is, boy, of course it is. That's what I'm here for: to get things done. But they've got to be done

45

through the proper channels, see? As the Chief Constable said, we can't have people taking the law into their own hands.'

'Would a law be broken then? If people went down and gave Drake a warning?'

Roscoe looked briefly perturbed. 'Not that I know of—oh no, no, no. But,' (he leaned forward again) 'as the Chief Constable said, things could get out of hand. That's what I'm getting at, boy—one step down the wrong road and all sorts of trouble could start.'

Robert smiled inwardly. Poor old Teg. It wasn't Plaid Cymru he was worrying about: it was the prospect of him losing the County Council chairmanship next year—even his Council seat, along with the hoped-for MBE and all that rubbing shoulders with the Chief Constable, Welsh Office ministers and Lord Lieutenants.

Robert stood, stroked the lock of hair from his forehead and stretched.

'If I hear anything then, Teg, I'll bear in mind what you've said. Stupid to let something like this spoil things for others, eh?'

He grinned and moved towards the door. Ten minutes after Roscoe's departure, Robert hurried into the pub.

'Plaid Cymru!' he scoffed, on reporting his visit from Roscoe to Meurig, Matt and Emrys. 'It's his own neck 'e's worried about, nothin' more.'

'But I thought he was Plaid,' Matt protested.

'*Was* is the word—you remember when he was first elected?'

The others looked blank. They were all in primary school at the time. Robert was sixteen, and helping his father run Teg Roscoe's campaign.

'Well then.' Robert leaned forward on the table. 'I remember 'im tellin' everybody who'd listen or not that he'd do all in his power to put Wales first. He'd never kowtow to an English government. Aye, everythin' was Wales first with him. Now look at him—shit-scared his friend the Chief Constable will screw up 'is MBE if the likes of us do what's right for us!'

Robert brushed away the lock of hair and sat back, daring the others to say otherwise.

Meurig leaned forward: 'So it's politics is it—this Drake business?'

'Don't be daft, mun!' Robert hoped his denial sounded convincing. 'What's Plaid or Labour or anythin' else got to do with it, eh? It's about direct action: people doin' what's best for them.'

Meurig leaned back and raised his eyebrows briefly, as if suitably englightened. Emrys took a swig at his beer to hide a smile. Matt looked puzzled.

'Teg's got a point, though, hasn't he? I mean, unlawful assembly, incitement to riot, that sort of thing . . .'

Emrys and Meurig exchanged glances. Robert was glad to divert away from party-political specifics.

'Bollocks, man. What's the harm in twenty or thirty people turnin' up in the street tomorrow night? Twice that number turn up outside the hall to cheer old Roscoe when he wins his seat.' He tapped the table surface with his fingers, in time to his words. 'All we're doing is turnin' out to give someone a warnin', right? Nothin' more—an' everybody'll be in the street, 'cept the two who go up to the door.'

Matt appeared mollified. Meurig asked quietly: 'So who'll go to the door?'

Robert swallowed: 'Well, me for a start—and you.'

Meurig shrugged: 'OK'.

Emrys was, in fact, the first to arrive outside the Drake's house at dusk the following evening. Feeling conspicuous, he slipped into the passenger seat of one of Alun Thomas's wrecks. Meurig was next, then Sally Evans bustled across to join them. A car parked outside the pub and three figures emerged to walk towards the garage. More cars and more people came from both directions along the road: there must have been thirty people gathered beside the garage when Robert came bustling up.

'Ready then?' Meurig asked.

'There's more comin' sure to be. We'll wait a bit.' Robert glanced anxiously about him. 'Where's Matt?'

Meurig shrugged: 'No sign.'

'The little shit's copped out.'

Robert sounded almost pleased. He surveyed the crowd, greeting friends and neighbours with a politician's polish. There had to be sixty present, and more were still coming. Meurig tugged at his arm.

47

'Come on then, mun.'

There was no sign of life in the Drake's house, but for a light in the hall shining out through the red, blue and yellow fanlight above the door. Robert fixed his eyes on the light and strode forward. The crowd followed, to bunch against the garden fence. The two men strode onwards, up the garden path. At the door, Robert raised his hand and rapped the cream-painted woodwork three times. A dog barked. Robert glanced nervously at Meurig, big and imperturbable beside him. A man shouted at the dog. A light came on above their heads. Robert was conscious of a sudden quiet as bolts were shot back and the door opened.

'What is it?'

Drake was brusque in jeans and grubby white singlet. He had not shaved for at least two days.

'It's, it's Mr Drake, is it . . .?' Robert began.

Alarm covered Drake's face as he looked beyond the other's shoulder.

'Here, what the bloody hell . . .? What're you bastards up to?'

The boldness of his words failed to conceal the fear in his eyes. He moved to slam the door. Meurig stepped forward, wedging a heavy boot against the door frame.

'Just a warning, Mr Drake—about your boy and his behaviour.'

Meurig's voice was firm and calm.

'Look,' Drake blustered, 'I've got better things to do than have you babbling on. Push off!'

Meurig held firm against another attempt to close the door.

'As I said, Mr Drake—just a warning, see? About the boy. Good night.'

He removed his foot. The door slammed. Robert almost toppled off the path as Meurig brushed past him and strode back down to the road.

'What did 'e say, boy—what did 'e say?' Sally Evans asked, grabbing at Robert's sleeve as he stepped through the gate.

'Nothin', Sal—nothin'.'

He forced a big smile. 'Now then, everybody, you've done your bit, and thank you. I doubt we'll have trouble from him again, eh?'

Robert appreciated the murmurs of approval and turned to find Meurig. He was already half way to the pub.

Nobody, including Robert, was particularly concerned as to what happened next: nobody noticed. Sally Evans was too busy making her husband's supper to see a white car draw up outside the Drake's house and leave half an hour later. She was in bed (and the pub finally closed) when Drake and his family drove out of the village. Only the next morning was the story put together by Betsan Harries at the school: the Drake boy was now in care, the rest of the family was in a caravan out on the coast.

'Well,' said Betsan, rounding off the tale, 'I'll doubt we'll see them back again.'

She spoke with a certainty borne of relief.

Nothing was certain in the mind of Councillor Tegwyn Roscoe. Backed up against a red-brick wall by a TV camera, he looked extremely pink and flustered. In the Tafarn-y-Bugail, the lunchtime drinkers watched and listened with jovial interest.

'Oh no, no, no,' Teg protested, his eyes darting from unseen interviewer to camera lens and back. 'We had been maintaining a most careful and considerate review of the situation. We acted entirely in the boy's best interests.'

A ribald cheer filled the bar room. Robert grinned. Teg was on the run. Perhaps he ought to make a claim for Teg's Council seat . . . The TV reporter pressed on.

'But Councillor, are you truly suggesting the removal of the boy into care had *nothing* to do with the events of last night?'

Roscoe looked suitably indignant, but his eyes were still shifty.

'Of course not!' he burst out. 'I, I, I mean I'm saying this: I believe two men did visit the house at some time, but that had nothing, nothing to do with the removal of the boy.'

Another jeering cheer filled the bar room. Robert grinned the more, straightening his back as he sat on a high bar stool. Twelve months to the next election: time enough to nurse some decent support.

'So you're trying to tell me,' the reporter persisted, 'that the presence of one hundred people, I'm told, had nothing to do with the boy's subsequent removal from his home?'

Roscoe's Adam's apple bobbed up and down as he swallowed hard. Robert sipped his beer. He could see himself in the Council chamber, fighting for the future of Wales.

'I'm sorry,' Roscoe suddenly snapped. 'I've made my statement, I can't say anything more.'

And with that, he scuttled away, the camera following his tweed-tailored back.

The cheers, jeers and laughter in the bar reached a crescendo. Hands and fists were slapped and thumped on every available surface. Robert downed the last of his pint, glowing with pleasure. As a semblance of quiet returned, he wrapped on the counter with his mug and stood to face the lunchtime drinkers.

'See, boys,' he announced. 'See how we've sent out a message for the rest of Wales? The law is still ours, boys—not the English parliament's, but ours. And Roscoe's sold out, boys—sold out to the English system.'

Robert sat down to an astonished silence. Griff behind the bar glanced anxiously around the room.

'Now, t'en boys,' he hesitated. 'It was only a bit of fun, eh? I mean, it was somethin' we felt necessary, see? Nothin' more, eh?'

Robert turned on him, a finger pointing at Griff's face: 'A bit of fun, eh? Are you sayin' that what *I* did last night was nothin' but a bit of fun?'

Meurig, silent until now, took half a step along the bar.

'What *you* did, eh, Robert?' he asked.

Only Robert caught the careful emphasis on the 'you'. Their eyes met. Robert swallowed and sat down. Meurig knew too much. He was a witness the others would believe above all else. A pool ball rattled into a corner pocket of the table. A dart hit its board with a dull thud.

'Aye,' said a voice from among the drinkers. 'Just a bit of fun, eh? No harm done, boys, was there?'

Robert slipped away, un-noticed.

Pennant

Pennant lay high on the flanks of Esgair Foel, its exposed, rocky acres an irregular pathwork of green amid the surrounding heather. For one hundred and twenty five years the farm had lived on borrowed time. Now, it seemed, that time was up.

For more than forty years, Tomos Edwards had tended his flock and a handful of suckler cows high on the mountainside with only his wife, cob and rough-haired collie as helpmates. Now the stock was gone all Tomos could do was ride out across his empty acres knowing—without bitterness or regret—that his son Robert was right to stay where he was. Pennant was no place for a young man successful in his own right.

At the highest point on the farm, Tomos reined in the cob and stared out across the timeless vista of the mountains, his vision blurred by tears which rose in his eyes but refused to fall. At the cob's front hooves, the collie lay panting, puzzled by the lack of sheep on the green sward before them.

'Aye, lad,' Tomos sighed, leaning forward to pat the grey cob's neck, 'it's been hard enough, and for all the talk, no-one will make it any easier.'

With that, he sniffed and turned his mount down across the fields to the farmstead hard against the stream head.

Pennant came into being—as such—in the late autumn of 1866, after Iolo ap Robert had looked up from his father's land in the Nantcoel Valley towards the virgin mountain and had decided his future lay there, on the bare, cold slopes and not in the stinking, filthy, dangerous valleys of the newly-industrialised south.

Siarl, Nathanial, Ebenezer, Evan and several others from the remote valley had already trekked that way, striking out across the mountains in search of the promise of riches to be found in the mills and mines which looked to the south and the sea and the burgeoning markets of the world. Few boys believed there was any future to be had in the remote confines of the Nantcoel Valley, and with Jacob already set to take over the farm from his father, Iolo saw little hope for himself deep amid the mountains. His father was keen for him to go: his father thought only of the supposed riches his son would send home to help support his bedraggled family.

But Iolo remembered the things told to him about the industrial south by the beggars and the paupers who had escaped its grip and returned to the mountains in vain hope of rebuilding their lives. They spoke of houses where two whole families shared a single room; of streets running with sewage; of water, red-brown and acid taken from wells. They told of drunkenness and violence in the streets; of deaths and maimings in the mills and mines; of men bent double in the bowels of the earth; of women and children scratching for coal beside them. They recalled the foul meat and adulterated foods they were forced to eat; the sickness and disease; the ever-present fear of death, and the money lenders who charged four times over for the price of a meagre funeral.

Iolo thought of all these things as he looked up onto the slopes of Esgair Foel and determined that his life lay there—as a farmer. And with the dream growing within him, he stumbled up the steep slopes through rough heather to a patch of rough grass through which an infant stream ran in a shallow, rock-filled gully. The presence of the grass promised soil deep enough to till, the stream a constant source of fresh water.

This was not a young man standing on the bare, cold mountain, but a boy of sixteen, ill-grown through lack of proper nourishment yet tough, wiry and determined. His clothes were the near rags of a linen shirt, trews and fustian jacket, its sleeves hanging an inch beneath his knuckles. On his feet were chipped and dirty clogs made for his larger father.

But in his mind, Iolo saw himself proud and strong amid his stock: a little house and buildings standing against the stream head, and bright green fields all around. He saw himself burning off heather, turning the soil and watching new grass grow as he pushed back the limits of his farm. And elated he went back down to his home in the valley—to his father's yard and its babble of calves and pigs and chickens. His father emerged from the low, stone, hovel-like house carrying a heavy, wooden pail.

'I bin up the mountain,' the boy announced, 'an' I reckon it'll do.'

His father grunted. He saw there was no future in the idea. The boy was best earning good money in the valleys, but it was up to him now. He would have to go, what with five other children to feed and clothe.

'You'd best take 'em up when you can, then,' his father replied. 'An' the donkey's yourn when I can spare 'im.'

'They' were the younger children, the donkey the family's only transport. Even Marged, not yet seven, would be of use in gathering peat and stones for Iolo's new house.

So, on wet days with the farmwork at a stop and with the donkey hitched to a sled, Iolo and the children went up the mountain. First they went past the stream head where Iolo planned to build his home and climbed to a peat bog high above. Marged cried in the cold and wet as they cut blocks which would dry in the summer sun and cover the roof of Iolo's home. Ffraidd would light small fires from damp, dead heather and bracken on which to heat peaty water. Aided by this scant warmth, the children worked through the day, stopping only to eat dried bread and hard cheese beneath a wan noon sun.

Throughout the summer the children cast wider across the mountain to gather stone for Iolo's home. Using branches cut from trees in the valley, the boys levered the larger rocks onto the sled with bruised and battered hands while Marged picked amid the heather for pieces no bigger than her fists.

'The little uns will fill the gaps between the big uns,' Iolo announced with the growing authority of a man determining his own future.

With the stones and peat gathered, he went into the woods to cut poles for rafters and from the timber man gathered up rough planks with which to make a door and window shutters.

Then, as dusk gathered on an early-November evening, Iolo, Jacob and other boys from the village went up the mountain and, in a frenzy of sweat-stained work which inured them to the bitter cold, they created a peat-roofed hovel in which Iolo—with simple ceremony—lit a fire as dawn broke across the mountains. In the village, as a damp grey light crept across the flanks of Esgair Foel, the peaty smoke was seen and noted and word went out that Iolo was now master of his own home.

In the hovel, the boys danced a little jig of jubilation, downed the last of the beer which had sustained them through the night and then slumped into an exhausted sleep on the coarse-grassed floor. Later, as the fire died away and the cold crept into their bones, they awoke and Iolo took up a small axe. Stepping out of his only doorway, he swung the axe to and fro with all his remaining might and hurled it down the mountainside. From where it landed, he stepped out in a circle round the hovel, so laying claim to the land he first planned to farm.

Years of unremitting toil then followed. Whenever possible, Iolo went down the mountain to earn what cash he could to buy his scant requirements. He slaughtered cattle, felled trees, ploughed fields and alone in the little hovel he sometimes cried, all but beaten by the enormity of his task, the cold and the loneliness, wishing he could return to the warmth and comfort of his family. Once or twice his father came up the mountain, grunted a grudging appreciation of his son's endeavours and went away again. Once or twice Jacob was released from his daily labours to help his younger brother. But twice each week, Ffraidd would come to cook a meal, wash his ragged clothes and bring brief cheer to Iolo's lonely life.

It was at chapel one Sunday morning that Iolo caught the eye of Lowri, so to begin a 'bundling' which lasted a full twelve months before she agreed to be his wife.

'It'll be 'ard, girl,' Iolo warned with simple understatement.

But Lowri wished to remain in her own domain, and there were few men of her age left in the valley from which to choose a husband. She said as much to her mother.

'If it isn't him, it'd have to be Gerald—or I go away.'

So the marriage was agreed, and seven children followed, Lowri working until the pains of labour racked her body. Three died at birth, the others drifted away. Only Ewart, the eldest, remained, confident of his right to succeed. News of the death of Edward in the Transvaal was met with sorrow but little comprehension as to events in the world beyond the valley.

Iolo died in 1900, aged fifty, leaving his son thirty acres of half-decent pasture on which to build and expand the farm. He had married Mary Evans from a farm like his father's, further west along the mountain. They worked hard and Pennant did well, until Britain slid into the doldrums of the Great Depression. Beset by mounting bills and a dwindling income, Ewart gained brief hope from news that the Forestry Commission was after five thousand acres of mountain land on which to plant a forest. He offered up Pennant and was refused.

'I'm sorry, Mr Roberts,' he was told, 'your land is too steep and the soil too shallow.'

To the west, where the mountain slopes were easier and the soils were deeper, Mary's father and his neighbours sold up with ill-disguised delight.

Deflated and defeated, Ewart went home to Pennant and told Mary they must give up. With the farm cob hitched to a wooden sled, he brought their belongings down to the valley and a waiting lorry, bound for a new-built Council house in distant Merthyr Dewi.

Ewart swore that no child of his would ever take up farming. But none of the three—two boys and a girl—ever showed the slightest interest in doing so.

Pennant lay empty for three years, the grass in its fields rank, its whitewashed walls greying and peeling. Nettles took root and thrived in the rough, rock-surfaced yard. Some said the place would never be farmed again, but in the fourth spring of its abandonment, Edward Edwards came over from the other side of Esgair Foel to buy the place for his third son, Mel. Once again the fields grew lush and green and the whitewash shone in the sun.

Mel did well during the Second World War and when Tomos took over in 1948 Pennant ran to eighty acres. Claiming grants to turn moorland into pasture, he pressed on. By the 1970s he farmed one hundred and sixty acres, ignoring as he went the growing protests that men like him were ruining the beauty of unspoilt landscapes with their neat fences and bright green fields.

'The buggers can't have it all ways,' Tomos would protest in answer. 'Can't have all the food they want and more while good land goes to waste.'

Three children came from his marriage to Eluned: Sioned, who married the heir to eight hundred Wye Valley acres, Bethan who settled for a Birmingham accountant and Robert, who proved a real child of the education regime triggered by the 1944 Education Act.

Having passed his eleven-plus, Robert went on to study agricultural engineering. Various jobs followed and with each he did that little bit better for himself and his new family. By the mid 1980s he was well settled as the marketing director of a major machinery dealership in Shrewsbury.

But as Robert prospered, so the fortunes of Pennant began to decline again. No longer did the Government look upon farmers with the benevolence of the previous forty years. In an increasingly free-market economy, men like Tomos began to struggle for survival as their incomes drained away.

At Pennant, Tomos checked his books for 1990 and saw he had earned no more than the £5,000 he had taken from the business for himself and Eluned back in 1980. He still owned the Land Rover he had bought that year; he could no longer afford a car for Eluned.

News of the plight faced by men like Tomos caught the media imagination and the protests began to grow: protests over the Government's cavalier attitude to upland and mountain farmers and fragile rural economies; over the destruction of rural communities and the loss of their historic culture. A Labour M.P. asked questions in Parliament and was barracked from the benches opposite.

In the short memory of the collective public mind, protests were voiced over the decline of important landscape values if farms such as Pennant were abandoned and left to go wild. Commentators and politicians now began to speak of the mountains 'becoming a wasteland'.

One day in late summer, three M.P.s climbed aboard a Range

56

Rover and, pursued by a posse of T.V. cameramen and newspaper photographers, drove up the long, rough track to Pennant on a fact-finding mission. That evening and on the following day, the nation was treated to evocative images of Tomos riding out with his grey cob and collie against a background of misty mountains, the sheep safely grazing around them. Great care had been taken to avoid any hint of the glowering conifer forest which all but encircled the farm.

But the sympathy of a nation could not save Tomos and soon after an advertisement appeared in the local paper: 'For Sale: Pennant, on the instructions of Mr and Mrs Tomos Edwards, who are retiring.' They lived with the euphemism as a handful of viewers came and went and never returned.

Eventually Tomos turned to the only man who might be sure to save Pennant.

'So what do you think then, son?'

And Robert paused and switched his mobile 'phone to his other ear as he sat on the patio behind his house. And in that pause he thought of his comfortable home with its double glazing and central heating; of his son and daughter, happy with their friends in the village; of Peter at Scouts and Melanie at Guides; of Jackie his wife with her own car and part-time job. He thought of the proposed holiday to Florida, now Yugoslavia was out of bounds; of the company car, company pension and company health scheme; of the five-minute drive to an out-of-town foodstore; of nights out with Jackie in Birmingham or Stoke. He thought of the comfortable village pub; of his golf and his cricket, and of the friends who dropped by for a beer and a chat.

And then Robert thought of Pennant: of the old farmhouse with its warped metal windows; of the open fireplaces and flag-stoned kitchen unchanged since before the War; of Jackie, remote from work and friends up the long, rough track. He thought of having to buy and maintain his own car; of the twelve-mile trek to a small supermarket crammed into an old bus depot; of the village pub with its bare floors and hard wooden chairs; of a life surrounded by conifers.

'See, I've been thinking son,' Tomos continued, in the vain hope that Robert might yet be persuaded. 'You could diversify, see? That's what farmers must do, they keep saying. You could turn the old buildings into holiday chalets and have caravans in the field. It's beyond me now, boy, but you're still young enough.

'Aye, diversification—that's the thing, they say.'

Tomos tried to sound positive. Robert frowned. The idea was ludicrous, to give up everything and hide up on the mountain, kowtowing to every Tom, Dick and Harry fool enough to think they could make a holiday out of visiting Pennant. He took a deep breath, shifted in his chair and answered in his best, brisk, business voice.

'I'm sorry Dad, but it's not on: it's not worth it.'

And as Tomos replaced the handset on its rest, he wondered that the comfortable, successful man in Shrewsbury should be his only son—the son of Pennant and its enfolding mountains, yet he knew that man was right.

Starting Again

Chris felt awful. Her head throbbed, her stomach churned, and she was on to her third mug of black coffee without noticeable relief.

Easing herself out of the easy chair, she flip-flopped through to the kitchen, her dressing gown hanging open, to reach for fresh asprin. Clarrie Davies was whistling as she hung out washing in the garden next door. Chris groaned: would she ever be carefree and seventy? Forty two years to go, but already she dreaded hitting the big Three-O. She gulped down a tablet. Girls of twenty eight should not celebrate birthdays—not when at odds with their lives.

She scuffed her way back to the chair. The cat yawned, stretched and shot her a reproachful glance from the comfort of the other chair. Chris envied his indolence. It mattered not where he lived or how he passed his time. Females meant nothing to him.

She rested her head against the chair back, her hair tousled round her face, her short nightie riding up her heavy thighs. She belched stale alcohol. Getting out from under Tony—metaphorically and literally—had been a good thing. So had the move to Merthyr Dewi— at first. Now she was somewhere and nowhere. The cottage was all she asked for as a home. She remembered her pride and delight in finding and buying the place; in stripping every wall, filling every crack and re-papering entirely on her own; in finding all those bits of furniture which said 'this place is mine'. All because she had fallen in love—with the cottage, the village and the gentle seclusion of the valley in which they rested.

Now the company was keen for her to to move, to send her back to England. Once she would have jumped at the chance: serious career girls never stayed still.

Chris yawned and clutched her forehead. It was all there, six years ago: that urgency of direction and purpose. Now it was absent. She eased herself out of the chair and up the stairs. A shower was called for. Naked in the bathroom she took stock yet again. Big bust, big hips, short waist and square jaw, with yellow-fair hair akin to fine spring wire. Plain and dumpy: 'sturdy' was the word her mother used in trampling all over the sensitivities of a sixteen-year-old. That was why Chris had stuck to Tony. How she had envied her friends, back in Swindon, with their apparently angst-free relationships and hints of sexual adventure! At least with Tony she had been relieved of the anxiety that men found her unattractive. So she had jogged along with him for nigh on four years. She shuddered, tested the shower water and stepped into the cubicle. Only her promotion and the move to Merthyr Dewi had opened her eyes to the dangers of that affair.

'But I thought we were going to marry,' Tony had whined on hearing her news.

'You never asked.'

'But I thought . . . well, I mean, we've been together so long . . .'

Then it had all come out: his plans for their home and years of dirty nappies.

Chris padded through to the bedroom. After the rows, the tears, the pleadings, she had gone, bought the cottage and settled to her new job. Two letters followed from Tony. She wrote in gentle reply. Then nothing, and she guessed why: someone else had entered his life. She was yesterday's woman, and freed of all guilt.

She sat on her bed in the back room. There were lambs in the paddock beyond the garden. A heron fished in the river beyond the little field. On the hill, the cows from Cefn Cantref fanned out across a field of fresh grass; a tractor worked nearby. Two buzzards drifted and cried on a warm breeze. Chris turned away: the light hurt her eyes. Tony may well have found another girl, but what of her? She winced as she wrestled with her hair.

Meurig: so Welsh she had never fitted into his life. She had tried learning Welsh, but it was no good. There was more to the way he lived than language.

Then Richard, who needed a mother, not a lover; Simon, the rabid Health Services trade unionist; Don, the odd-job builder with a degree in economics; Will, the supermarket baker with a wife and kids at home, and Ben, the drop-out who railed against the super-market ethos, but relished the food and wine she bought at staff discount. Six men, six years—and to what end? They had done nothing more than fill for a time that empty space within her life.

Chris gave up on her hair. Meurig lived at the heart of local society, Richard, Simon, Don and Ben way out on its perimeter. Even Will, with his wife and children, felt set apart.

'Why Wales?' she once asked Don, as he talked of his need for a simple life. 'Why not France or Germany?'

'I don't speak their language.'

'You don't here.'

'That's my problem.'

She knew what he meant.

Chris headed downstairs again. Bel was at the back door.

'Hi kiddo, happy birthday!'

Chris groaned inwardly. Bel was slim and lithe and well past forty. In jeans and tee-shirt, she went without make-up and bra with all the confidence of a twenty-year-old. And she was married.

'What's up?'

'I got pissed.'

'Oh.'

Bel helped herself to coffee.

'You can't run away from it, kiddo—getting pissed solves nothing.'

They sat in the back room, Bel crossed-legged on the hearthrug. The cat laid claim to Chris's lap. She knew Bel meant well: they had been through this before. Wrapped up in the business of making good the cottage, she had failed to heed Bel's warning.

'You'll find it hard to make out round here, kiddo. More than half of them speak another language, don't forget. Of the rest they're this and that. I don't know half the English round here. They're all tucked away in their farms and cottages, doing their own thing. You won't find soul mates round every corner.'

Now Chris understood what Bel had meant, those five long years ago. Bel was her only real friend. Most of the girls at work were married. Those who weren't kept to themselves within the Welsh milieu. It was the same in the village. Only a determination to be her own woman had kept her going.

Chris picked at a knot in her hair. She was close to tears. Six men in six years. She had fooled herself into believing sex was the only intimacy that mattered: conned herself into assuming she could find a man whenever she wished.

Bel looked up: 'So what's the answer, kiddo?'

Chris shrugged.

'Then get out, kiddo. Get back to England's green and pleasant. If they want you to go, go!'

Chris leaned forward: 'But I can't, Bel. Could you go back to somewhere like Swindon? Where could I buy a cottage like this, in a village like this?'

She was frightened of England: frightened of going back into a society which lived only to make and spend money. Swindon, with its ring-roads and motorway and ever-expanding housing estates—it scared her silly. She rarely visited her parents.

She challenged Bel: 'Would you go back?

Bel shuddered.

'See!' Chris was triumphant.

'But I've got the kids and Geoff,' Bel protested. 'And we've got the shop. Anyway, it would be far easier for you to go back than us. What would we do, after selling the business? Where would we live, with two teenagers to house? You're single, and you've got a job.'

'What job?' Chris all but asked.

Ben was to blame for that: Ben the drop-out who lived in a broken-down cottage, but relished the food and comforts bought by her labours. He hated supermarkets; hated the way they wielded their influence over the expectations and habits of shoppers, and rode roughshod over the commercial culture of small communities. Chris and her colleagues, Ben contended, were 'human automatums responding to the diktats of centrally-processed statistical analyses which forbade the exercise of individual expression and initiative.'

'You're a puppet,' he insisted, tucking into salmon and wine.

Chris eased herself out of her chair and lodged her bottom on the window sill. Ben was right in his way: she was locked into a system, a system which could pick her up and plonk her down wherever it chose.

'Did you ever want a career?' she demanded of Bel.

Bel jumped up and went to make more coffee.

'Not really. Twenty five years ago, kiddo, it was enough to make the effort—show willing. When you tucked yourself up with a new hubby, everybody understood.' She returned with full mugs. 'Now women are expected to have careers and marry. Even then you are not considered a 'real' woman until you've had kids and farmed them out for somebody else to screw up at £3 an hour.'

She sat at the table.

'You don't agree with that?'

'Do I heck—do you?'

'Not really.'

'So what grabs you most: career or playing mum?'

Chris turned and stared out the window. Doreen was herding her kids along the path between the gardens and the paddock. Married at twenty and now Chris's age, she was born, raised and married in the village. She epitomised the womanhood assumed of Chris by Tony.

Chris and Doreen rarely spoke. Doreen was guarded: did she disapprove of Chris's lifestyle, or envy her freedom? Was Chris, with her men, a threat to Doreen's certainties about marriage, mother-hood and life? Chris turned away: she would never know.

'I'm not sure.'

Bel drained her mug and stood up.

'Well, kiddo, think about it—hard. I've got to go.'

Chris walked to the end of the garden. There were seventeen lambs in the paddock now, two just born. She watched as they struggled to their feet and sought their first milk, the ewe anxious and attentive. Chris felt a stirring inside her: a tingling in her nipples. Was she right to deny herself the role for which she had been created? Could she fulfil that, and pursue a career? No one today would question her right to do so. She just lacked one essential ingredient—the right man. She sighed, and turned back to the cottage.

She prepared a light lunch: toast, pate and tomato. Damn Ben for sowing those doubts. She wanted to stay in the cottage and village:

she resented being moved by the company. If only she had told him to mind his own business. Instead, she had acquiesced to keep him sweet. It kept him happy and willing to share her company, and her bed. It helped drive out the loneliness.

Chris washed her knife and plate, and made coffee out of habit. On her bed she stared at the ceiling, a hand on her stomach. Did she want children? She needed the option to have them: the assurance that when the time came, she would be able to do so. That time was running out: she was nearly thirty. She sat up. She must go back to England and start again.

Downstairs, the 'phone rang. Bel was excited.

'Hi kiddo! Fancy a party?'

Chris grimaced: 'Where?'

'At Lionel's—Lionel Maescelyn.'

'Never heard of him.'

'See what I mean? You can live around here for yonks and never meet half the people who're your so-called neighbours.'

'What's he do?'

'He's into organic veggies—and does the accounts for people like us. He's a nice bloke—nothing flash.'

Chris grimaced again: 'All right—when?'

Maescelyn stood against a side road, two miles out of the village. Chris viewed with dismay the elderly Morris Minor, battered Citroen, tired Lada and dirty Volvo in the yard behind. She was in no mood to have fun with hippies, or whatever they called themselves these days.

Lionel proved younger than expected. Balding and stocky, he carried still the pinkness of his previous office life. The house was well cared for and comfortable, the guests smarter than anticipated. Chris began to relax. Lionel poured white wine in a well-appointed kitchen.

'So you're in the food business?'

He handed Chris a glass. She blushed.

'The tiniest of cogs in a very big machine.'

He smiled a friendly, open smile and chatted on. He believed in organic food production: he wanted to see organic foods widely available in supermarkets. But too many producers kicked against the supermarket ethos. They also expected premium prices for their products. They were wrong. They had to strive to achieve the volumes, price and quality customers demanded. At the end of the day, the punter with the trolley set the pace—not the supermarkets.

'If people want scabby apples, they will buy them.'

Chris agreed. Lionel nodded, a little grimly, towards his other guests.

'But try telling them that.'

Chris smiled: 'OK, I will.'

'Good girl.'

She was embroiled with a tall, thin, bearded man with bad teeth. Supermarkets were out to kill off organic foods: they sold what suited them, not what the public wanted. Chris argued back. Market research and in-store wastage showed that the public did not want apples with scabs, over-large cabbage, stunted carrots and slug-nibbled spinach.

A hand clutched hers, and drew her away.

'See what I mean,' Lionel whispered.

'Don't I just.'

He laughed. 'You did well.'

He squeezed her hand and did not let go. She did not object. He was a nice man. He knew what he was doing, and why. She smiled to herself: a pragmatic idealist. And he was only thirty four.

Chris sat on the bed, warm and pink and damp beneath her wrapped-around bath towel. She reached for her mug of coffee.

'So you really are on your own?'

Lionel grinned: 'Irrevocably divorced and very, very single.'

The hairs on his chest were greying. Track suit trousers had sufficed for his trip to the kitchen while she showered.

'For how long?'

He was propped against the headboard, hands clasped over his balding patch.

'Two years—on both counts.'

'Do you ever see her?'

Chris needed to know. He smiled.

65

'Never. No wife, no kids: no access hassle, no Child Support Agency commissars. I've been a lucky man.'

'Did you want children?'

He reached out and grasped the nape of her neck.

'Let's forget our turgid pasts, eh? Let's celebrate the glorious present.'

Chris kissed the end of his nose and giggled.

'I'll screw to that, any day.'

The die was cast: she was on her way back to England. A two-week course and then off to wherever the company pleased. Chris was not entirely happy.

'But what if they send me to Bootle or Burnley or somewhere like that?'

She was in her kitchen, preparing a meal. Lionel lounged in the backroom, watching through the doorway.

'Look, if it worries you that much, do the dirty on them.'

Chris was shocked. 'What do you mean?'

He came to the doorway and leaned on the frame.

'Go on their course—make the most of them, and then resign.'

Chris froze, a saucepan poised above a gas ring.

'You're joking!'

Lionel picked a piece of carrot from the pan.

'I'm not. The greater your skills, the greater your chances of finding other work.'

He popped the long, orange slice into his mouth.

'But where?'

'Here.'

She leaned against the work-top, the pan still in her hand.

'But I'm a specialist in personnel work. The only chance of work like that around here is with the County Council, and they want Welsh.'

Lionel grinned: 'I meant, with me.'

'You?'

He laughed, took the pan from her and placed it on the ring.

'Why not? People are always asking me about staff problems. They sidle up to me as I'm sweating over their books and ask how they ought to sack somebody, arrange interviews, handle NVQ training schemes—that sort of thing.'

Chris turned her back on the cooking.

'But it wouldn't pay—not down here.'

Lionel placed his hands on her waist.

'We could share expenses.'

'How?'

She felt her heart beat faster, her mouth go dry.

'Well, an office and office equipment for a start. Then light heat, house maintenance, food, bedding, that sort of thing.'

He was grinning like an excited child. Chris raised her hand to her stomach and pressed it gently.

'You mean . . . ?'

'Exactly!'

They ate and planned and went to bed.

During the following week Chris admired all the more Lionel's skill and confidence in mapping out their ideas on paper. Armed with a calculator, he worked through a maze of figures, turning imagination into hard fact. Her confidence rose: so what if she used the company course to further her own personal ends?

They were in bed in her cottage. Down in the village men laughed, chatted and called out as the pub closed. Once the sound of their camaraderie left Chris feeling very alone and isolated. Now she cuddled up to Lionel, and felt good.

'Tell me,' she whispered. 'What if babies become mixed up in all this super-professional freelance stuff?'

Lionel frowned: 'Babies?'

She raised herself up on one elbow to look down on him.

'Yes, babies: do you want children?'

She saw both consternation and horror cover his face, and in an instant knew why Lionel's marriage had failed. She turned away with a sudden convulsion, as if from a hand swinging down to slap her face. Self pity and fear engulfed her. But even then she knew, as tears filled her eyes and began to dampen her hair on the pillow, that she would certainly, doggedly, start all over again.

Not Nice but Necessary

A caravan was parked outside the shop, brilliant white in the mid-afternoon sun. Edith grimaced and sighed. One now, hundreds later. She carried her tea tray through to the front room. A man plodded past on the coast path, intent in shorts and heavy boots, a rucksack on his back. Edith straightened her back and bit into a biscuit. How she hated the coming of summer.

Back in the kitchen and rinsing her delicate china in the sink, Edith looked out towards Penlan. Six caravans were already parked in the field behind the farmstead. Come August there would be one hundred. The same at Cefncoed, and in the woods behind the village music would blare out from the log cabins late into the night. The air would stink of barbecues.

It wasn't really a village, just an assortment of cottages and houses scattered along a lane which dipped down into a shallow valley and out again, crossing a narrow stone bridge as it did so. Under that, the stream which came down from the head of the valley at Coomb End ambled through marram-grassed dunes to spill out across the beach just where the beach road petered out in a tumble of broken tarmac and concrete.

Edith sniffed, folded a glass cloth over the chrome towel rail and returned to the front room. It was a lovely view from her little cottage on the Southern Headland: of the bay and the beach curving round Stott's Head, a mile to the north; of the untidy, tussocky dunes and the hamlet with its oak-clustered backdrop reaching all the way back to Coomb End. It was a view she loved with the quiet certainty of one born into its midst.

It was time to pop down to the shop before it closed. Soon it would be inundated with sweaty, sun-burned bodies demanding ice-creams, postcards, beach balls and all the other flotsam and jetsam essential to modern holiday-making. It was no good, Edith decided, as she checked her floppy-rimmed felt hat before stepping out onto the coast path: something would have to be done about the annual tourist invasion.

The beach was all but empty now. Edith sighed. How she hated seeing it packed to its limits with prostrate, sun-scorched bodies, people in silly hats playing ball games, screaming children and scolding parents and dogs running wild. Radios competed with ghetto-blasters and the innane chimes of ice-cream vans. A walk across the sands to the base of Stott's Head was impossible. How she loved to clamber over the ragged rocks at the base of the Head on the ebb of the tide and walk all the way up to Carn Point, where rough steps gave access to the coastal path and her return to the village.

Even up there, on the path, there was no peace in which to amble at leisure, spotting coasters and ferries far out to sea or musing on the timeless inland landscape of fields and woods undulating towards the distant, blue-grey Preseli Mountains. Edith sniffed contemptuously as she strode out towards the shop: no, even on the path one ran into ramblers, earnest and always hurrying in sturdy boots, khaki shorts and backpacks. And the thought of their feet in those thick woollen socks after a long hot day . . . Edith shuddered.

At the lane edge she waited for a car and caravan to pass her by, obedient to the imperatives of the returning tourist traffic. After a long walk on the beach and path, she would often pop into the shop for a cup of tea and chat with Molly. Together they would sit in the little back room, sipping tea, exchanging gossip, their ears alert for a ring of the doorbell. Now, with the tourists coming, their chats would have to stop for the summer. Molly was too busy to pass the time of day—and implacable in the face of Edith's oft-voiced protests about the annual tourist inundation.

'There's no money to be had from the likes of you popping down here for your weekly half of butter and quarter of tea, woman,' Edith was told, quite bluntly. 'And you should know especially. What I makes in three months is good for the next nine, an' that's the sum of it. Like it or not, it's the tourists which keep me here—nothing else.'

And Molly was right, Edith reflected, awaiting her turn behind a young man in tee-shirt, shorts and sandals. Already the shop front was festooned with beach balls and windmills and buckets, with more profit in each item alone than half a dozen four-ounce packs of tea.

At one time, Edith's mother had run the shop. It was a place in which to live and produced a bit of extra income on top of what Father earned from the sea. Boats once cluttered the bay: heavy, black-tarred open boats, rocking on their moorings as the village men prepared and mended their nets upon the beach. Tar tubs hung over driftwood fires and tumbled piles of lobster pots spoke of a village which lived and worked with the sea to survive. Those were the days before the War, when Edith shocked the village by rowing out in her father's boat to fish alone, returning home with her hands and face red-raw from the salt and cold. She was never shy of hard, sometimes unpleasant work. During the War she drove bomb-laden lorries, day and night, to the bleak bomber bases of Eastern England. Milking the cows at Cefncoed was almost a respite during the twenty years that followed.

In the pub in those days, fishermen and farm hands alike chuckled their admiration for the women over pints of thick, dark ale poured from a pewter jug. Now strangers talked of cars and caravans, pleasure boats and videos over halves of pale, fizzy lager. To them, Edith was the dotty old lady in broad-brimmed felt hat who went about with a plastic bag picking up litter with a five-inch nail rammed into the end of a bamboo cane.

But no one else did, Edith told herself. No one else tried to keep the village tidy. They were too busy making money out of the tourists to worry about the mess their visitors left behind. So she went about the dunes and the street to spear the wrappers, cans and plastic bottles, and emptied the inadequate litter bins which the Council seemed to think would empty themselves. It was too bad, she would complain to Molly. It was never like that when fishing was the lifeblood of the village and people had respect for their community.

'Now,' she would say, 'we are over-run with strangers who care nothing—nothing—for us or the place we live in. So what if it's ruined? They just go elsewhere.'

'And you,' she often felt like adding, 'you and those who live on them do nothing to protect the village.'

So Edith, doughty and seventy, returned to her headland cottage from the knick-knack-laden shop and awaited the annual invasion. Something would have to be done, she told herself, looking out across the beach and houses from her kitchen window. Something more than picking up the litter—a token gesture if ever there was one, for nobody really seemed to care whether she did or not. Something which would make them stop and think.

The breeze off the sea was turning chilly. Edith laid and lit a fire. Perhaps later that evening she would go out for a walk—after dark.

*   *   *

In the first light of a mid-August morning, a handful of early risers opened their eyes and sniffed the most revolting smell. Ben Williams, on his milk round, saw the cause and felt the bile rise in his throat. Horror-struck, he saw the black and awful sight upon the beach, and ran to raise the alarm. At first, Ben did not wish to look too closely, but in the stream beneath the bridge the evidence was there for all to see. With a terrible and deadly menace, a thick, turgid slick of raw sewage filled the stream bed and spread in a black, revolting fan across the sands as the tide ebbed far beyond the headlands.

Police cars arrived with whining sirens and flashing beacons. Fire tenders followed in hot pursuit. Strings of red and white plastic ribbon fluttered in the breeze to fend off the masochostic curious. Water company vans arrived in a great dyspeptic flurry. And little boys gathered at the bridge to hurl stones at the revolting flotsam with ghoulish delight. TV cameramen and press photographers jostled for the best positions and reporters bent over notebooks and mobile phones.

But as the sun grew stronger, so the smell became a stench. It permeated every nook and cranny of the cottages, every corner of

71

the caravans and every crevice in the cabins. It cloyed in the backs of nasal ducts and clung to every clothing fibre. By ten o'clock, cars packed the exit from the village, piled high and battened down in a flight to fresher airs. Residents with no compelling reason to hang around slipped away amid the throng.

Edith looked down on the tumult and confusion from a safe and fresh-aired distance, at ease in a salt-bleached deck-chair in her salty, scrubby garden. The breeze came warm and fresh from the sea, the sky was cloudless, and the coastal path, running alongside her garden fence, was free of ramblers. Only Molly, 'phoning from the shop, disturbed her peace.

'Oh it's terrible, dear, terrible,' came the obvious news. 'They reckons half a million gallons were let out at the works at Coomb End. The police says it was vandals—opened the tank gates last night, they did. I shouldn't go too far from home today if I was you, dear. Anyways, the police are going round house to house, making inquiries. I tell you, Edith, it'll be the ruin of me, it will.'

Answering a knock on the front door, Edith found a young constable standing on the step, sniffing the air with the expression of a wine expert savouring a particularly fine bouquet. Edith invited him into her small front room. A whiff off the appalling sewage odour hung about his uniform. His questions were brief: had she been out yesterday evening? Yes, because evenings were the only chance she had of enjoying an undisturbed walk. At what time, and where? Had she seen any strange vehicles around? Edith smiled.

'Oh dear, Constable, the village is full of strange vehicles this time of year.'

He blushed slightly: she was right, of course, but did any particular vehicle catch her eye? Or did she by any chance see a person or persons behaving oddly? Perhaps a young man (or men) worse the wear for drink?

Again the smile: 'I am sorry, Constable. All holidaymakers seem to behave strangely to me and, of course, people do get a little drunk at times. But thank goodness this is not the sort of place which appeals to young people. We mostly cater for families, you see.'

With apologies, the constable departed. Edith switched on the

72

lunchtime television news. The sewage disaster dominated. The reporter at the scene had judiciously stationed himself on Stott's Head, up-wind from the thick, black smear which lay in the glutinous fan shape across the beach behind. With equal circumspection, a police chief inspector—with his buttons and badges shining bright silver in the sun—reported from a nearby spot that the beach could well be closed for a week or longer, and then roundly condemned this 'wanton act of mindless, terrible vandalism'.

An expert on enteric diseases rose to the occasion with horrific predictions as to what dread diseases people might catch if they used the beach or sea before it was safe to do so. A water company spokeswoman (safe in a distant studio) stoutly defended her company's record of environmental improvement works. An environmentalist launched a counter-attack, while a bewildered man from the National Rivers Authority tried to pick his way between the verbal flak.

Closer to home, Richard Morris, the District Council's director of tourism, all but wept as he spoke of the enormous damage done to the local tourist industry—a point proved by the sight of caravans queuing to leave their pitches in the fields at Penlan. Finally, Councillor Harold W. Roberts appeared, incoherent and purple with rage and looking all the more like an angry turkey cock in horn-rimmed glasses. Edith smiled and switched off the television.

In the shop, Molly abandoned her brave attempts to keep the wheels of commerce turning and headed up the coast path to Edith's clear-aired sanctuary.

'It's the stench, dear,' she moaned, and then warmed to the morning's gossip. 'All the caravans have gone, dear—and the people from the cabins. Megan Jones says people are cancelling bookings right left and centre—even some for Christmas. And they reckons that if the wind stays in the west, it could be a fortnight before the stuff is cleared right away. I tell you, dear, it'll be the ruin of us—the ruin of us. Our best month of them all, and nothing—not a penny I've taken since half past eleven!'

Edith offered tea, lunch ('Only a bit of salad, mind') and sympathy, along with a change of clothes. Even Molly could not disguise the

73

pong which clung to her, and was grateful. 'I reckons we're much the same size, aren't we dear?'

A fresh wardrobe was found and Edith returned to the kitchen. Out at the water's edge, men in thigh-length waders were ramming long poles into the sand with JCBs, and stringing nets between them. On the sand, astronaut figures in protective clothing busied themselves among sewage tankers, their pumps whining under the load. The sirens were silent, but the blue and yellow beacons of the police and water company vehicles still flashed, the cars and vans scattered along the short beach road and among the dunes. And but for a handful of vans caught up in the clean-up operation, the village street was empty.

Edith smiled and filled the kettle. So what if she had denied herself the pleasure of summer-evening walks upon the beach? The tourists had put paid to them already. Of course it wasn't nice, what she had done in that extra-dark hour before dawn, up in the woods at Coomb End. Not nice, but necessary, for it was worth every minute of that dark and messy struggle to have the village at peace with itself again: tidy and quiet and free of the innundations of modern summer life. She poured water on tea leaves that couldn't keep the shop in business.

Upstairs, Molly was singing lustily and loudly as she changed her clothes.

Little Woman

Three messages awaited Ben Phillips when he returned to his desk after lunch. The first confirmed the time and date of yet another meeting between officers of the District and County Council economic departments and their Welsh Development Agency counterparts. The second confirmed that Malcolm Garrett had been granted planning permission to extend his pottery. And the third simply read 'Ring Mrs Thornby re museum idea.' A Tenby telephone number was scribbled beneath.

Ben slumped in his chair and groaned. There were times when the plethora of local, county and regional initiatives designed to boost the West Walian economy seemed entirely geared to inter-agency meetings at which those attending out-bid each other for the kudos of helping create the most (non-agency) jobs. After eight years with the County Council economic department, Ben sometimes wished he had the guts to go out and set up his own little business. At other times, he shuddered to think of the mess he might make. Malcolm Garrett came to mind.

Long ago, Ben had decided that three types of English person moved to Wales. The first came in pursuit of a career or work, the second aimed to live off a private income (be it investments, a pension or social security) while the third aimed to pursue a business venture in an un-stressed, un-spoilt environment. Malcolm Garrett was one of the latter.

A former crafts teacher, Garrett had bought a house and buildings in the middle of nowhere and set himself up as a potter. At first he had enjoyed moderate success—enough to take on two staff, but then he ran into trouble. In a bid to help bail him out, the County economic development department was now advising on the re-structuring of his business. This involved securing a loan, through which Garrett would be able to extend his work and showroom area. Privately, Ben deemed this an act of lunacy, since Garrett enjoyed little or no passing trade and produced goods which were only mediocre. But he was stuck with the rescue job—on the orders of his boss.

Taking up a biro and notepad, Ben decided Garrett could wait, and dialled the Tenby number. He wondered without enthusiasm what Mrs Thornby had in store.

'Hello!'

The voice was clear, warm and upbeat. Ben imagined a woman in her fifties, elegantly dressed and with greying hair wound into a neat bun. She had to be energetic and entirely in control of her life. A little bossy, maybe.

'Mrs Thornby?'

'Speaking.'

Ben mellowed a fraction. She at least sounded business-like.

He mellowed all the more as she began to reveal her plan. It was to open a museum of rural life. She possessed a large collection of rural 'bric a brac'—bits and pieces of farm and rural crafts equipment dating back to the last century, and wanted to open a museum. She had studied visitor data to the Pembrokeshire coast for the past five years, spoken to her local planning department about access and building conversion requirements; found someone to design the displays and publicity material and was now looking for a suitable property, preferably on the A40 near Haverfordwest where her project would be easily accessible to visitors along the South and West Pembrokeshire coasts. Ben smiled to himself and wondered how he could be of use to someone so organised. He asked as much. There was a brief, uncertain silence.

'I just felt I needed a second opinion—that's all. I've spoken to the bank, but honestly . . .'

In that moment, all her confidence appeared to have ebbed away. Ben sensed a certain defensiveness in her tone. He arranged a meeting and knocked at the door of Mrs Thornby's rented cottage at ten o'clock prompt the following morning. The place was small and white and neat, the car in the driveway likewise. It was with a start, as the house door opened, that Ben turned to face a woman dressed in jeans and tight-fitting black tee-shirt, her brown hair cropped shorter than his and her ears decorated with small studs,

76

one on the left and three on the right. A fifth glinted in her right nostril. She was oval-faced, with a slightly snubbed nose, smiling mouth and large, brown eyes. In his confusion, Ben felt the eyes should have been violet.

'Mrs Thornby?' he hazarded.

'That's me—come in.'

She stepped aside and Ben found himself in a large living-room-cum-kitchen. Neatly laid out on the table were files and maps. On chairs, the sofa and the floor lay several pieces of the collection, each neatly labelled.

'Take a seat.' Mrs Thornby gestured towards a dining chair. 'Tea, coffee, fruit juice?'

Ben did as commanded and opted for coffee. Mrs Thornby seemed entirely at ease with herself and her guest. As he studied her shapely rear view, Ben came to realise she was no older than his thirty years. He felt suddenly inadequate—a mere theorist facing up to a professional.

They spent three hours working through Mrs Thornby's plans and figures. The collection had come from her grandfather and she had added to that by going to farm sales, house clearances and poking round junk shops.

'See this,' she enthused, reaching for a curved, wooden-handled blade. 'It's a corn hook. Since people were using mechanical reapers by the end of the last century, and judging by the wear on the blade, it could well be more than a century old. Certainly the manufacturers went out of business in 1910. I like that,' she grinned, 'researching the history of things, getting my facts right. People can be so sloppy.'

Ben studied her papers and was suitably impressed. Her visitor data covered numbers, spending levels, age profiles, amusement preferences, socio-economic status and so on. She produced cash-flow charts, capital costings and a raft of other figures, followed by sketch projections for the presentation of the artefacts, a cafe and a children's play area. On a map, stickers denoted the most popular visitor centres, with the roads leading to them highlighted in black.

Ben sat back, stunned: 'What can I say?'

Mrs Thornby looked childishly anxious: 'It is all right is it?'

'Of course it is—it's excellent—I can't fault it.'

Ben swallowed and cleared his throat. 'Although there is the question of . . .'

Mrs Thornby laughed and regained her usual bouyancy: 'Money?'

'Yes.'

All that, too, was accounted for. She explained in further, thorough detail.

'Then all I can say is the very best of luck.'

Ben stood.

'Are you really sure it's OK, then?'

She sounded surprised and not a little bewildered.

'It's the most impressive presentation I've seen in my eight years with the department.'

'Truly?'

Ben twigged that beneath the gung-ho confidence there lay a deep uncertainty. For a crazy moment he wondered if her husband knew about the scheme: was she on the run with the old man's pet project? He sat down again.

'As I've said, I've never seen a better presentation. In fact, I was wondering who . . . Well, who showed you . . .?'

'Who?' She sounded a little offended. 'Nobody—I figured it out for myself. My ex used to talk a lot about business planning—cash flows and so on—but in terms which suggested it was all above my little head. I suppose I just absorbed it, then transplanted his millions down to my thousands.'

Ben laughed: 'Then you are impressively absorbent!'

She smiled and looked somewhat relieved.

'Thank you. Look, please stay for lunch.'

It was a plea rather than an invitation. Ben accepted. She hummed as she produced toast, pate and salad, rather like someone recovering from a moment of great anxiety; like someone who has realised that a great fear was entirely unfounded.

As they ate, she again expressed a mix of surprise and relief that Ben should find her work so impressive.

78

Again he reassured her: 'With the right site you can't fail. By the way,' he added, 'I feel I can't keep calling you Mrs Thornby.'

She laughed: 'You've avoided calling me anything for the past three hours! It's Alice, by the way.'

She held out a hand across the table, which he shook with due solemnity.

'And I'm Ben.'

'And is the use of Christian names part of your development plan?' She was laughing at him. Ben blushed.

'No . . . well, I mean calling people over fifty Mr or Mrs is OK, but . . .'

'Not the likes of me, eh?'

They both laughed.

Back in the office, Ben found his colleagues—once they were aware of Alice's approximate age—keen to assume (entirely in jest, of course) that more than a business discussion had taken place that morning. Moreover, beneath the teasing, he detected only a cursory interest in Alice's plans.

'Her research and planning were absolutely superb,' Ben told his boss. 'The best I've ever seen.'

He was treated to a frown: 'Well, just be careful. Some of these women are all very good with bits of paper, but when it comes to running a business . . . By the way—Malcolm Garret, how are things with him?'

Dave Roberts, across the room from Ben, swore that Alice (or 'your little woman,' as he had dubbed her) must have used a consultant. When Ben hit back that she made the Malcolm Garretts of their world look like bewildered schoolboys, he was told (somewhat sharply) that Garrett was 'OK'. Ben wondered if this was in reference to Garrett's business acumen (for what it was worth) or his enthusiasm for rugby and the pints which followed. Very quickly, he learned to keep quiet about Alice. He was upset to have her brushed aside as 'his little woman.' Saying nothing made life easier.

Ben's only real input into the museum project was to find a ten-acre small-holding alongside the main A40 into south and west Pembrokeshire, with the enormous advantage of lying against a long lay-by created out of a road-straightening scheme. The house and building lay at the foot of a low hill and faced south. The house was unchanged from before the second World War, save for the addition of a kitchen and bathroom at one end. Alice decided the extension would form the basis of her own accommodation, so allowing her to use the house for exhibition purposes. For the time being, she would sleep (and relax when possible) in a caravan alongside the extension.

By the time the builders moved in, Ben felt more at home in the caravan than his own flat, which was how he came to be wandereing around the yard one Saturday morning as Alice went about other business.

'Look at this, mate,' the foreman demanded as Ben walked past. 'What the heck are we meant to do with this, eh? And she's gone gadding off.'

He indicated a crumbling stone on which a cowshed roof beam rested.

'Jack the beam up and replace the stone,' Ben suggested.

The foreman shook his head: 'Can't see how she's going to make out with this lot, mate—not without you around to sort things out.'

Ben said nothing of this exchange to Alice, but clearly the foreman's attitude was getting at her.

'The bloody fool,' she stormed one day. 'I told him, quite specifically, to re-lay the wash-house floor with at least an inch to spare for the flagstones on top. What's he done? He's laid it right up to threshold level. Told me I'd be better off with tiles—not flags. I mean, Ben—is he a total idiot, or am I?'

And then she looked suddenly downcast.

'It is me, isn't it? I mean, I'm not used to this sort of thing—men laying concrete and the like. The most I've ever done is repaint a bedroom, with instructions from my ex.'

Ben protested that the foreman was a total fool: he had no right to ignore specific instructions. She was entirely in the right. Alice looked at Ben, her brown eyes large and troubled.

'But he did ignore me, didn't he? And just because I'm a mere woman, isn't it?'

Ben tried to protest otherwise, but she had stepped forward, linked her arms round his neck and burst into tears. With her face pressed into his shoulder, she whispered with an unnerving venom: 'Oh God, I hate men!'

The museum opened in the third week of June, Alice organising a press visit to coincide with that from local primary school children. It was a slick move: pictures of delighted tinies made the local, regional and TV news.

Yet several times during the first fortnight she became agitated. Viewing a near-empty car park one damp Saturday afternoon, she asked Ben: 'Was my homework really that good?'

Then later: 'What if all those people who said they liked visiting museums and places of historical interest only said so because they felt they ought to?'

Ben chuckled and tried to reassure her: 'Does it matter? What people say they like doing and what they actually do so often depends on what's available. I go to amateur operatic productions because I can rarely get to Cardiff for the professional stuff. I'm sure once people know you are here, they'll flock to your gates.'

Alice gave him a look which suggested she accepted his humouring but not his reasoning.

It was during those first quiet weeks that Ben became more aware of Alice's parents. They had moved to the area on retirement and it was as Ben sat sipping a cup of coffee in the deserted cafe one Saturday morning that Alice's mother joined him.

'Are you sure Ally is doing the right thing?' she asked.

'But of course,' John assured her. 'Come the school holidays, you won't be able to move in here.'

However, Alice's mother was clearly thinking of other things.

'It was such a shame with her and Greg. I thought they had settled down so happily and then Ally got it into her head that he was

81

treating her like some sort of servant and heaven knows what else.'
She sighed. 'I suppose it will be too late by the time she gets this out
of her system.'

'Too late for what?' Ben asked carefully.

'Why, children. Greg was so keen to have children.' She sighed
again. 'She's thirty one already, you know, and women can't be too
careful when they get past thirty.'

Ben took a sip of coffee. Alice's mother was watching him.

'Do you want children, Ben?'

She was asking him to say 'yes'. He cleared his throat.

'I'm not sure . . . You see, Ally and I . . .'

As Ben had predicted, the holidays were hectic. So much so, the
museum venture was adjudged the Best New Small Business in
Wales. Ben was delighted, but refused to travel to Cardiff for the
televised awards ceremony. He had to retain a modicum of
professional detachment. Besides, he was keen that no one should
be left in any doubt that Alice was the true star behind the venture's
success.

At work, his stock had risen considerably. He was still assumed to
be the real power behind Alice's diamond-studded facade, and it
was on the back of this belief that he was able, with some authority
and effect, to argue that Malcolm Garrett was a lost cause. Garrett
proved so by going bankrupt as Alice welcomed her 15,000th
visitor.

Ben and Alice were all set to marry in the spring, when he would
give up his job and work with her. They worked well together, and
Ben was quite happy that Alice should remain the driving force
behind the business. He was intelligent and sensible enough to
realise he was not a natural 'front man'. Alice operated with a verve
and panache he could never match.

She had come a long, long way in less than a year, Ben reflected,
as he lounged in the caravan awaiting Alice's return from the
awards ceremony, the television no more than a back-drop to his
ruminations. Yet no further than he had expected. He was sorry,
though, to see the studs go, and her hair was longer now. The tight

tee-shirts and jeans had given way to well-tailored, tweedy suits in what he called 'hedgerow colours'. She had, in effect, become as professional in her appearance as she was in her mind.

Ben stepped through the little 'tunnel' he had created between the caravan and a new doorway in the kitchen wall as Alice drove into the yard. The car door slammed with a ferocity borne only of anger and she burst into the room with tears in her eyes.

'What the hell's the matter?'

He was alarmed and puzzled as she flung her arms round his neck and sobbed freely onto his shoulder. He guided her to an upright chair at the table, sat her down and reached for the kettle.

'Tell me,' he pleaded as he spooned coffee powder into mugs.

'Oh God,' Alice mumbled, 'is it all worth it?'

'All what?'

'All this.' She gestured in the direction of the museum. 'All the work, the worry, the hassle.'

Ben placed a mug before her and let her take her time. She sighed.

'I'm sorry love. I've been so pent up all the way back. Poor Mum and Dad, you'd think I'd won an Oscar. Mum got quite tipsy—kept telling everyone how clever I was to do everything on my own.'

'She was right. So what went wrong?'

Alice sipped her coffee.

'Oh it was great—wonderful—until we went into the hospitality room afterwards, when this slob came up—he'd won an award too— and put his arm round my shoulders. "A word of advice, love," he said, "get a man in to run your little place—someone who can build it up a bit, make something of it. It would give you more time with the punters then—the mums and kiddies. They like a woman's touch." I mean, Ben . . .!'

He laughed: 'You should have told him to get stuffed.'

She sniffed: 'I did, sort of, but he just chuckled and patted my bottom.'

'That wasn't all . . .' He watched her keenly. She was trying to tell him something else.

'No, it wasn't.' She sipped her coffee and avoided his eyes. 'No, I could cope with that slob, but then the producer came up.' Alice gazed down at the table top. She was speaking while other thoughts ran through her mind. 'She was younger than me—a "right on", new woman type. She said how sorry she was that you weren't there: how you must have been a tower of strength and what a reassurance it must have been to have you help and guide me. My God, Ben.' She looked up, her eyes red and damp. 'When an intelligent, responsible woman executive like that . . .' Alice shuddered, her voice fell to a whisper. 'You know, it makes me wonder if I'm marrying you just to conform . . . to be the little woman, the way people expect me to . . .'

Ben suddenly felt himself go cold with fear.